D1607393

The Truth About Dragons: An Anti-Romance

Books by Hazard Adams

FICTION
The Horses of Instruction
The Truth About Dragons

CRITICISM
Blake and Yeats: The Contrary Vision
William Blake: A Reading of the Shorter Poems
The Contexts of Poetry
The Interests of Criticism

EDITOR
Poems by Robert Simeon Adams
Poetry: An Introductory Anthology
Fiction as Process
William Blake: Jerusalem, Selected Poems and Prose
Critical Theory Since Plato

The Truth About Dragons: AN ANTI-ROMANCE

BY *Hazard Adams*

HARCOURT BRACE JOVANOVICH, INC.
NEW YORK

The lines from the poem "Sweet Dancer" are reprinted
with permission of The Macmillan Company from
Collected Poems of W. B. Yeats, copyright 1940 by
Georgie Yeats, renewed 1968 by Bertha Georgie Yeats,
Michael Butler Yeats, and Anne Yeats; and with permission of Mr. M. B. Yeats and Macmillan & Co. Ltd. The
lines from Hopkins' poem "Spring and Fall" are reprinted
with permission of Oxford University Press from *Poems
of Gerard Manley Hopkins.*

ISBN 0-15-191320-X

Library of Congress Catalog Card Number: 70-134569

Printed in the United States of America

A B C D E

M

for anyone who has wished to talk with a dragon

The Truth About Dragons: An Anti-Romance

Preface to the Diary

It had been a long time since man or any other animal had come up the old dirt road. There was a period when it had been used now and then by forest rangers, but fundamentally it was only a firebreak. Some years ago I had gone to great trouble to construct a barricade with an imposing warning sign a mile downhill to the west. So I was surprised when the camper truck appeared one afternoon at the crest of the hill and proceeded to bump and rattle off the road nearly to the edge of the tarn. The noise alerted me, and I came to the aperture and looked out.

How annoying it was! Hardly before the truck had stopped, three children were out and into the tarn, swimming and splashing around and making a fearful racket. The mother began to set up camp adjacent to the truck, and the father busied himself with the accessories of their vacation: a canoe came down from the roof, two old inner tubes appeared from the back, a tent was pitched in the rear, lawn chairs and a barbecue emerged to the side, and a transistor radio went on full blast. Mother did a wash. Dad took out a fishing pole. The children screamed. They had set up for a long stay. They had already tossed three Pepsi cans into the brush.

I was extremely nervous. I don't like to be penned up for more than a few hours, even if I am fully occupied with my work or my art. Now I could not emerge until they packed up all their belongings and went away. I turned, perplexed, and loped back through the tunnel to the Outer Hall, where I had been dabbling at an easel. Of course, I could not concentrate on the canvas. I could not even look at it seriously. I was worried that the children might stumble upon my home. In the tarn they were ill-humored. They looked like thorough explorers. I pondered upon my anxiety.

Within the bounds of our restraint we are inventive; soon I had considered the situation and adopted a plan. It would go into effect in the night, before the campers had gone to sleep, but not before the children were bedded down.

When the time came I was ready. I swam quickly through the underground stream, emerged into the murky depths of the tarn, and shot to the surface. Treading water at tarn center, only my eyes and the crown of my head above the water line, I surveyed the camp site. There was a lantern flickering inside the camper. The tent was dark. I began to circle the tarn, keeping near to shore, making the water lap. As I swam faster, the water lapped harder.

I managed to create an adequate commotion. The camper door opened, and Dad emerged with a big flashlight. I ducked under the surface just before the light scanned the tarn. He must have stood there for some time until the water subsided, and then, perplexed, called it a night. When I arose he was gone, so I circled again and again. This time Dad reappeared with Mother. I watched them surreptitiously, an old floating log. After pacing about nervously on the shore, the two of them went back to bed. I repeated the process three more times; with each new effort I managed to rout out one more human being, until at last all five stood at tarnside observing the curious waves. Then, when all was ready, I shot from the depths to the center of the tarn and, with my mouth just at the water's surface so that almost nothing of me showed, I blew a large fireball straight up in the air, and another, and another, until the air above the tarn was warm and the Oaks around it illuminated. I imagined the Oaks laughing.

It was enough to send them off. It wasn't quite enough to send them without their tent, which they quickly stuffed into the camper. It wasn't quite enough to send them without the canoe. But they did leave a number of other items behind: the rather badly smithed barbecue, the clothes drying on the line, one supermarket lawn chair, and my prize—a plastic tape recorder. Of these items the last was by far the most elegant. The barbecue couldn't have withstood one firebreath, we don't appreciate chairs, and the clothes, of course, were of no value except as rags to clean my brushes.

For several weeks after bringing the tape recorder back to the barrow and leaving it casually in the Great Hall near my favorite sleeping quarters, I would merely glance at it now and then. It wasn't the best recorder in the world by any means. It was intact, however—complete in its case with auxiliary tapes. One had only to press button A and speak. But I resisted the desire. Not that I had nothing to say. It was simply that I had never before collected objects for use. I had considered it impure to do so. I am, like all my kind, a—well, a human being would call us "compulsive" collectors and aesthetes. My cairn of glass bottles contains examples from the earliest settling of California. It is a representative and valuable collection, dredged up from the bottoms of streams and lakes, old wells, and long-abandoned garbage pits. I am very proud of its most prized items—the Fiskerville Glass Works commemoration of Jenny Lind and "General Taylor Never Surrenders" back to back in green clouded glass with "The Father of His Country." In one special alcove I have displayed these objects, arranged historically from the earliest blown whiskey and tonic bottles to later brilliantly colored cut glass. I have chosen to locate this collection near the treasure along with my Cord, my Marmon, and the Ultimate Model T. I call it the Ultimate T because it is my synthesis of numerous relics driven by their owners into the hills and simply left there to rust. I am still creating this object, transforming human productivity and its resultant junk into order and art. I must discover some way to obtain from Sears its yet missing parts.

Then there are the cans, throwaways, and cartons—they are far less interesting as collector's items, but I gather them, too, keeping them separate from the bottles, of course, and from the plastic containers. Somehow it's hard to imagine that the plastic objects can ever achieve aesthetic value, but that is what they said of Simon Rodia's junk. So I collect them and bury them here and there near the mountain barrow. I can dig up any object should need arise; I cannot bear to display them all to myself.

All over the world other dragons are acting as I am—committed scavengers through all recorded history, preservers of culture, of history, of art and beauty, against men who make it, and would destroy it, who lack the capacity to wait, to sleep long, to breathe slowly, to guard what they should treasure. Having observed the abrupt decline in the quality of junk and relics, I have reason to think that we have overstayed our time.

Today I have overcome my aesthetic scruple and succumbed to my urge to speak into the machine. It is a matter of vanity. I intend to keep a diary and to make it, like

7

all dragonistic acts, an artistic whole. Is it merely that I wish to leave my own record? Perhaps, but I convince myself that the real temptation is the challenge of literary creation. In the fine arts my achievement has not been inconsiderable, but I can no longer improve upon my technique. I choose the recorder because writing is cumbersome for clawed creatures, even those as dexterous as we. I shall say all that I say with a prophetic aim, for art is prophecy, and prophecy is simply the telling of truth, not how it shall be, but how it is and must be or could be. I sense that if I am to speak it must be soon.

March 7

Call me Firedrake. It is the human name my grandfather adopted after his father was so named by the bard. He liked the poetry of it, and so do I, and so did my mother. Eterskel was Great-grandfather's dragon name before the bard's story maligned him. There have been thousands of years of those bardic lies all the way back to Apollo's alleged victory over Delphyne. I snort black soot at every one of them. No man alone has ever defeated a dragon, has ever scored against us with a sword.

In the poem, you'll remember, at the crucial moment when old Beowulf is in real trouble, he is aided by a warrior named Wiglaf, who actually—I can hardly bear to say it—kills the dragon. Well, here's the truth, as my grandfather tells it. He was strong, but small then, about twenty-two feet at the time, and very frightened because of all the noise and shouting, and the men with big helmets with horns protruding out, and the women huge as Amazons and as muscular of leg, with round, dragon-embossed shields. They came on horseback, circling the mountain like Indians around covered wagons. They whooped and hollered in Geatish, and old King Beowulf sat to horse on a mound nearby, simply watching and directing the attack. Great-grandfather was supposed to come out; then everyone would charge on him. So, Beowulf's friend, "Wiglaf" in the poem, was in truth a whole damned army of Geats and their awful wives, with catapults and flame throwers and spears and anything else that men had invented by that time for the torment of one another and the animal kingdom in general.

If Eterskel had remained hidden, maybe they wouldn't have managed to do him in by force of numbers. But Eterskel (or The First Firedrake, we call him) was angry, and he had always disliked Beowulf, for Beowulf was an incorrigible braggart. Not that Eterskel wished to avenge Grendel's death. All that business, my grandfather says, had been absurdly overplayed afterward by the gleemen, who were in Beowulf's pay. Grendel and his dam were ogres, *not* dragons, and the ogre is simply not in the dragon's fighting class. But it got so the bards Beowulf commissioned to write up his exploits implied that they *were* dragons, or at least blurred the distinction. Well, Grandfather said absolutely, and the whole dragonish lore says absolutely, that those folk were merely ogres. Giant ogres, maybe, but not dragons.

Of course, Beowulf was a strong young fellow in his prime and conceivably could have done in two ogres. But *not* if Grendel had been a real fire-breathing dragon! Why, getting up that close he'd have been singed to a crisp, as if some Druid had put him in a wicker basket and torched him. No, even with the hootin'-hollerin' Geats pounding around the mount on their wild furry horses with their horned helmets and painted faces like the savage human beings they were, even with all that, Eterskel in his prime would have done them in, but he was old—nearly nine hundred and fifty—and slow, with only a few consecutive breaths of fire in him, and his distance wasn't what it once had been. And my grandfather, though still small and without experience, had passed all the trials and was nearly ready to take over. Eterskel could have hidden, but he was just plain angry at the idiotic noise and the impertinence of this old white-haired mad king who was using the episode for political gain. The Druids had been giving Beowulf a bad time over some tax matter, and Beowulf needed a good victory and a bit of a carnival to get the people's minds off what the Druids were saying about his plans to offer only modified fief reform. The old fellow wasn't going to get very close to the action, though; he was merely planning to take the credit in the bardic annals, and all of the political gravy.

So Eterskel came out of the barrow with a huge and final burst of energy. His thirty-five feet had been tightly coiled to spring, his dragon wings were flapping and his nostrils smoking. The horses whinnied and scattered from the circle, and the big women howled, and Wiglaf (all five hundred and fifty of him-her) found himself-herself-them in disarray. It was the surprise of it. Perhaps none of them had ever actually seen a real dragon. Perhaps many had not even believed in us. No doubt many had been humoring the old king, and some had assumed they would go out on an uneventful bivouac and return and the bards would

call it a dragon-killing. Eterskel made a single lunge and
two or three firebreaths do the job. Right at Beowulf he
went, wing-flapping, springing, loping, while the braver
souls among the Geats, who were a tough people, stunned
momentarily, collected themselves and started throwing
everything they owned at him.

Beowulf saw what Great-grandfather was about, but it
was too late. The first breath burned Beowulf's *byrny* of
mail and took off his beard. The second got the horse, and
then Eterskel threw a loop around the old man and
squeezed the life out of him right then and there. With his
diminishing firebreaths he fended off most of the attackers,
but an anonymous spear had delivered a deep, blinding
blow to one eye and injured his brain. He had just enough
strength and presence of mind to make it to the big tarn,
and he went far down under, pursued to the water's edge
by the screaming women of the horde. Grandfather never
saw him again, nor did anyone else. In fact, Grandfather
was hiding in the tarn not far away, a young dragon, as
I said, only his eyes showing, crocodile-like, among the
reeds.

Of course there was a big thing in the poem about
Beowulf on his deathbed instructing Wiglaf to enter the
barrow and take the treasure, but those are lies. Eterskel
had known Beowulf was after the treasure. Perhaps the
Geats did enter the barrow. But dragons don't live by firebreath alone. The treasure was hidden underground miles
away from where Eterskel performed his final valorous act.
It had been his ruse all the time. And if those foolish Geats
did enter the barrow, all they found were a few cheap
chalices and pendants that had been very popular among
the young human beings that year. They were made of tin

and decorated with fool's gold, and cheap glass. (If there's one thing a dragon can't resist, it's collecting things.) The Druids were intensely interested in holding on to law and order at the time, for the Geatish women had been agitating to re-establish the worship of Cerridwen and the female priesthood; and since they didn't intend to embarrass the Crown now that Beowulf was dead, the Druids arranged for the poets to go on with their story the way it's told even today. It's a good piece of fiction, I suppose, from the human point of view. But hardly prophecy.

It would take tape after tape to right all the wrongs human poets have perpetrated against us. I think of St. George. Do you know that the first St. George was a whole shipload of Greek sailors on a drunken spree, who just happened to run aground near Joppa and found three very nice-looking young Greek girls in a field of goats and were after them like a bunch of satyrs when Draiko, a young dragon who was hidden nearby watching and trying to decide which one of those young things he——? Well, when he saw this he simply chased those Greeks back to the shore, whence they came (as we say), blasting them with fire again and again (he was a very fit dragon at that time), and those that escaped had to go by sea, and by their own arm strength. There was no dragon killed, nothing of the kind. After his long swim, one of the sailors, a self-styled poet named Perseus, blew up a whole bunch of stories about dragon-slaying—with himself as hero. It kept him in subject matter for years, but only we dragons remember him as the author. He's mixed up in human myths as a warrior-king now, and scholars and psychoanalysts are putting all sorts of meaning on the tales, all but the real one——

Which is that there *are* dragons, we are not allegorical, and no single hero has stood a chance with us. Not one. Human beings do not believe in us much these days. We have become more solitary and seldom reveal ourselves, for the human being is a much greater danger than he once was. His technology has come to match ours, and he could destroy one of us with any number of weapons. We can still hide effectively, though, because that same technology has imposed upon him a technology of the mind: to him we are no longer creatures of reality. To him we are merely creatures of the libido, the id, what have you. He does not search for us where we may be found. Our stealth and his machine myth of himself and of Earth provide what protection remains for the treasures.

March 8

Learning to shut off this recorder took a bit of doing, because of my large claws. We are able to do many difficult things with them, but they *are* large, and this machine —well, a dragon would have designed it more efficiently, even for human use. But that's part of its built-in obsolescence, I suppose. In a few years, I'll have to open up a hi-fi, etcetera, alcove.

I had better admit that what I hinted at is true: this record is made not simply for art's sake but because I am not sure that the epoch of dragons and men as we know them is not nearly ended. And I desire that a dragon's story be told for those who follow, whatever may be their nature—a higher intelligence capable of deciphering my words, perhaps. I am aware of the big earthmovers crawling slowly back from the coast. From Santa Barbara, Ventura, Oxnard they come, like huge—well, monsters, breathing out the stench that maketh smog, eating up and regurgitating huge gobs of Earth, flattening and squaring the hills, changing the run of streams, destroying the watershed. How can it be that they will not come finally to my mountain, to my tarn? They will scrape at the upper levels and discover first the relics I collected when the Indians left. Then the Spaniards' helmets, their sea chests and the decaying fabrics they brought for barter. Experts will come from the Huntington Library, from the Midwest and the East, to marvel over these ruins and erect mistaken theories. They will dig deeper and find the *Big Little Books,* the *National Geographics, Pic, Look, Life,* and the old Ovaltine mugs and decoder rings, the ruptured ducks, and old marksmen's medals. But the treasure, no! By night I move the treasure farther northeast into the Sierra Madres, where for a century now I have been planning its final repose. Deep, deeper in Earth, so deep that men will not yet find it. But will they not advance upon it again, and then where will there be to hide it? Unless the human era should end.

March 10

I rested yesterday from the work of many nights, and in the evening I spoke with Feuerkugel, who holds the northern sector as far as the Canadian border. He may be one of the successful survivors when the time comes. We spoke of this, of how the hills there are protected by a more severe winter, how—— Oh yes, you do not know how we communicate over such vast distances. First, let me explain a number of things about us. Our culture is totally spoken. It takes far too long to write, since our minds work very quickly. Our prodigious memories render books unnecessary. Man thinks his mind is like a computer or a computer is like his mind (he has not decided which and he had better do so soon), but we are *really* electronic, though we encompass our mechanism with spirit; and our memory bank is not clouded by a censor. Most of us have learned to read with great speed; we are excellent at languages. Indeed, as I have tried to suggest, we are the guardians of culture, of the arts; and we would be guardians of the sciences, except that much of human science is simply a part of our nature. We take it for granted and do not think of it as some Other to guard. We have not had to *learn* mathematics, we *are* mathematical. And as for much of what human beings call engineering, what is its use to us? We make our own fires, we are well insulated, human diseases do not strike us, we are not by nature hung up about death. Indeed, we find most human learning except the arts and loftier speculations about the universe something of a bore. Our conversations, generated by our own power over thousands of miles and by methods of modulation unknown to man, have gone on for centuries. Our only problem has been, in recent years, the human ham operator. Occasionally a conversation between Portland and Fresno or elsewhere jams our signals. How dreary those conversations are! Most human beings simply have *nothing to say to each other;* their communications reduce themselves to inane talk about how good so-and-so is coming in, and I heard Ukiah real clear yesterday, and what real fine kind of a thingamabob I've installed in the whatyou-callit. We dragons will at least survive the adverb.

When Feuerkugel and I talk we often compare human and dragonian civilizations. Our view of the former is substantially influenced by contemplation of what we scavenge. We listen to the radio, watch some television, and pick up the newspapers a few days late, but our deepest insights into human life come from trash. Sadly enough, the magnitude of trash long ago overwhelmed us. We have not been able to collect it all and bury it for centuries. Man: the animal rational? The *animal symbolicum?* No, the *animal discardans*. This matter has become a fearful obsession with Feuerkugel since San Francisco began sending its garbage by train up to his country. Last night he suddenly injected into a rather profound metaphysical discussion the question, "Who discarded the moon?" San Francisco is getting to him. All important discourse he converts into the language of disposal. Dragon lore does so, too, of course. It tells that Earth and the planets were formed from the vomit of the glowing celestial Draco, whose fiery breath then lit the stars and blew all things into their whirling paths. Our most ancient stories prophesy the return back into him of everything that Draco's great sickness caused to be discarded, but only when dragon culture has recollected and reshaped the world in edible form. This is allegory; you can interpret it on several levels as you wish. But no celestial dragon would eat up what lies about on Old Earth now. Dragon lore was referring to an Earth made into spirit by dragon art. It would not be singed one bit by the fire in Draco's mouth. What hope of that is left?

We discuss these things, Feuerkugel and I, the two westerlymost dragons in addition to Nasha, who tunes us in from Alaska now and then. Centuries ago the fearful Knäckerune, the great sea dragon-poet, from his lair in Scotland made into verse as part of the *Great Blerwm* the story of Draco that we all have learned. The prophecy at the end, after a recounting of the epic struggles of the dragons Daniarood and Stuhoard with the Scottish kings, known as the *Dragononian,* refers obviously to my territory. I render it thus:

> First fared the human kind,
> Formers of styrofoam.
> Thick though their layer,
> Short be their stay.
> High in the western hills,
> Shorn of their soil,
> Eroded, denuded,
> Barrowed before man,
> Dragons dug deep,
> Trove up the treasures,
> Chests cached for caretaking
> Grails of the goblin world,
> For delectation
> At Draco's last dining.

We guard what man must not find, shall not despoil.

March 11

I have not been quite honest. I should mention another matter that has influenced my decision to speak. One night about three weeks ago I was wandering about looking at dumps and other harbors of refuse near the coast, not suffering from our "compulsion" so much as employing my interest as an excuse for a pleasant stroll. The night was soft and warm, and I was enjoying a respite from the underground work that had occupied my time of late. I was promenading along a chain-link fence rimming a dump when, at the turn of a corner, I saw ahead of me a man wearing dungarees, an old elbow-patched jacket, and a beret. He was moving along briskly, talking to himself, or singing, or perhaps chanting. I had a little trouble making out what he was saying until I realized that, whatever it was, it came in a definite tetrameter. Once my ear was tuned to the verse I realized that the gentleman was chanting lines about a giraffe. I edged up behind him and heard him launch into Eliot's "Hippopotamus," then add a stanza or two, haltingly, to the giraffe poem, which I took to be his own. It was a light piece, and I was amused by it. I decided to speak to him. Naturally, he turned about, startled, and I talked as fast as I could to calm him, saying he shouldn't be afraid, I had been interested in his poems and thought we might converse, though dragons rarely spoke to human beings.

For a moment he considered full flight, but he could well see that I would easily catch him if I so desired. So, quite shaken, I'm afraid, he answered edgily that, ahem, it was not typical of his walks that he should happen upon a dragon, and that he hoped I would forgive his surprise. He eyed me carefully. I observed that he had been speaking Eliot, and he smiled slyly.

"It is true," he replied, "that you are remarkable creatures, students of the arts."

I nodded gravely.

"It is by no means true of all *our* species," he said. "I would hope that the record of you dragons is better."

"It is," I replied.

"Good," he said. "I would guess that your art is prophetic in the old Biblical sense. Am I not right?"

"Indeed," said I.

"Then what do you have to say about the fate of the West? Is it written out how we shall come to our corporate end? If not, your prophecy is worthless. It is coming, it is coming, by quake, pestilence, famine, or war." And he offered several very depressing lines on freeways, which seemed to put him into a state of great agitation, for he felt it necessary to recite Blake's "Cradle Song" immediately afterward. When he had completed his recitation and taken a few deep breaths (we were not walking together but loitering at a corner of the fence), he fell into thought. We stood there for a time, and then he began:

"I do not know how long your story may be, longer than mine, perhaps, with maybe as much despair about mankind. Nor am I acquainted with the subtleties of your civilization—beyond what I have been able to imagine when I have thought of dragons and how they must live and what they are in the great irrationality of things. But I have concluded, as a poet and artist who has spoken a word on the egret, the emu, the raccoon, the grey wolf, unicorns, and dead dogs, as well as other beasts that don't come to my mind right now, that it would be futile to speak about or for the dragon, since clearly according to my imagination, clouded and human as it is, the dragon can speak well in his own behalf. He can quite adequately instruct us as to his functions, bodily and spiritual. He can no doubt speak to us in such a way as might save us; the fire of his prophecy might sear us in the spirit. He is a wonderful, a fabulous beast, chaste of spirit, strong of tail, thick of hide, bejeweled. For all of these reasons, I have never written a dragon poem.

"But why has he not spoken to us, why has he remained hidden from human sight? Reticence? Incompetence at verse? Hatred of man? No, my friend, suspicion! He believes that we will tell the white whales, he believes that we talk too much, that we could not understand his message. But there is little more time, and he must speak soon and instruct us how to be saved."

I did not know how to stop his rambling. He shouted now that man would not hear even his own poets. It would take more than a poet dressed up as a huge fire-breathing dragon to make it through to man these days, if ever; and only a dragon himself, reciting prophecy in the meter of his choice, would have any bearing on events. Poets were a small and vocally ridiculous minority, but one dragon was a vast minority, and vastness was all anyone attended to. Would I care to accompany him down the coast to call on the President? We could proceed together through the hills and compose the epic as we went along. He could help me with some of the transitions, perhaps. He suggested that we might use Jeremiah as a model.

How to get away from this mad poet? But suddenly he was calmer, and he looked me in the eye and said, "Hell, it's not your responsibility, anyway. But," he brightened with the thought, "we could get in the gate. You could say you were the new Assistant Attorney General, and we could meet the Chief Executive on the beach and . . ." But at that moment he simply leaned against the fence and began to laugh. I waited for him to recover, but he just kept laughing. Then he sank slowly to the ground and sat there laughing and laughing. He seemed to have forgotten I was there. I watched him laugh for a while, and finally I slunk away. I headed back for the barrow. I remember at that moment thinking that maybe some dragon ought to speak out after all.

March 12

Hard work all night with the carrying of the minor treasures—the lockets with the pictures, the great dragon brooches, many small pieces—from station to station through the mountains by tunnel during the day, over the final ground by stealth at night. Then finally there will come the worst, most boring work, the closing of the ways, the filling of the old passages, to leave no trace of my retreat.

March 15

It has been three days since, busy with the moving, I have spoken into this machine. I have worked totally underground because of the strange thing that has happened. On the twelfth, at early dusk, I set out for the second tunnel with the Lesser Chalice. Hot all day it was; I had adjusted my thermostat twice, but now the cool dew had begun to fall. There was a film of it on the undergrowth, the trees were still, and I heard a mockingbird up in an

Oak. I stopped to listen, its many songs were so pleasant. I coiled there quietly waiting for it to repeat itself, when another answered and spurred it to greater efforts. The natural music of such birds gives us dragons great pleasure. Wagner was not wrong to include a dragon in his opera, though I must say that he did not provide it with dragonish lyrics. A vulgar beast he made of it. Tolstoy was right. A man cannot successfully imitate a dragon.

Suddenly I realized that I was not listening alone. About fifty yards off, on a huge rock near the tarn, were two human beings. Strange, for I had seen none like them in a century—not since the awful days of the gold rush, when some half-crazed, ragged prospector would stumble far south into these goldless hills. The young man was in black cowboy boots, black cowpuncher pants, a black leather jacket, and over his face and head—masses of hair. He sat on the rock, a black Nazi cap beside him, a can of beer (aluminum, I know) in his hand, his legs crossed like some Indian yogi, his back against that of a tanned, black-haired girl of about three hundred (were she a dragoness), wearing an Indian band across her forehead and blue jeans and matching shirt, sitting there yogilike too. They were listening in the falling dusk to the same bird, now engaged with its mate in a sort of contest. The sky was red through the smog in the west toward Lompoc, dark in the east, the shadows filling the canyons, hiding me. I was very quiet, frightened that I would be discovered carrying the Lesser Chalice, which is of great importance and must be kept out of human hands.

I wondered whether they were alive, they were so quiet. Then suddenly the mockingbirds stopped. It was silent in the hills. The bulldozers and earthmovers had hours before ceased growling toward the sea. Only the crickets sang. The young man turned, and the girl fell back softly on his lap. He put his hand to her cheek, then to her breast, and kissed her briefly. She arched her back, and he kissed her again as she lay there. Neither had spoken. It was my fault entirely that I was discovered, for at that moment I found it necessary to clear, very quietly for a dragon, my throat, and I smoked a bit through my nostrils. I crouched, lizardlike, as close to the ground as I could, but that wisp of smoke was my undoing. It was the girl who heard me. She raised herself on one elbow and looked fifty yards more or less right into my eyes. Her companion rolled onto his back and watched the sky or maybe just lay there with his eyes closed, when she said, "Hey, like that's a dragon over there! Hey, he's, like he's smoking!"

But lover boy is lying on his back, watching the heavens—old Draco in the sky maybe—and wants her to de-freak herself right now, I mean, look there's no dragon that isn't friendly like Disney says, so why panic? Clearly he was no materialist, as I could tell by the way he hardly revealed any matter under all that hair. (We dragons have no hair, you understand, and the hair fetish this fellow seemed to have didn't annoy me; somehow it just wasn't relevant.) He wouldn't buy my existence over there as a dragon, and who would, from this chick who was probably flipped on hashish and feeling very Oriental and *wanting* a dragon to show up somewhere or other and do the things Oriental dragons are supposed to do in her dreams? (Yes, I've heard all the human lore of Eastern Dragonism, all the way back to the primal yin and yang and the plenitude of explanations of how it's best done.)

"Hey, look," she said, shaking him; her voice had

changed into that of the worst harpy or Morrigan I had ever listened to in the old days around Lough Corrib. "Get up, man, and see the dragon," she rasped out very slowly, pronouncing each word clearly in his ear, once she found it. Well, the tête-à-tête proceeded along these lines, with him telling her to come on down with him where there were only those great stars and planets all around, like, maybe millions, all in his head—he was slowly getting them all in his head—and would she stop, please stop pronouncing all those words so he could UNDERSTAND them. And she was beginning to get serious, still harpylike, in her all-blue shirt and tight jeans, standing now and looking down at him, then hopping around him like some odd bird, flapping her arms, and then in a little fit stamping her foot and saying, "Goddammit, Beautiful, it's a d-r-a-g-o-n." Spelled out in sarcasm. And so, very slowly, with immense show of indulgent patience, he stretched, yawned, wiped his eyes, took out his gold-rimmed glasses, raised himself on an elbow, said, "Where's your dragon, Goneril, my daughter?" which I thought a reasonably deft touch. "If the whore of Babylon isn't riding its heads, it's going to be a big dis— Holy Jesus!"

You are wondering why I hadn't scurried away before this and left the poor dear arguing for her absurd vision and saying, But, I mean, it was so vivid, and it even smoked once, and it was all jewels and beauty (for young women really like us). Well, I suppose that's partly the reason. I hadn't seen a young chick like this alone for about one hundred and fifty years. It was then a young Spanish girl out of the mission at Santa Barbara came wandering far into the hills and took me by surprise grazing in a meadow and I decided to talk calmly with her and send her away friends. But it's bad for them, because they seem to have to go back full of this EXPERIENCE. I suggested she should explain it all away by saying she'd eaten some strange mushrooms; it would be better all around. She cried, of course, poor thing. She'd taken an instantaneous liking to me, and she saw it would be quite a distinction to be a dragon's friend. She didn't understand that it must go no further than that. Or did she? I doubt that she had ever known of mermaids. Well, the mermaids didn't exactly come from the sea. No, we sent them there in the old days, for the young things were not adaptable to land. But there's almost nothing of that now that there are fewer of us and most of us are under *Wyrd* to protect a treasure at all costs. With our *Wyrd* come certain disciplines, or *Geis,* so there are not many mermaid sightings these days.

To tell the truth, it's really HARD WORK with a dragoness, but with those young human women one can see that it would be possible to coil all around them and get every bit of their softness and their sweet smell and not have to worry about having some dragoness loop your tail and squeeze the hell out of it or fog up your jewels with her fetid smoke-breath. And then they always kick and claw when they're on their backs. It's a natural reflex. All creatures of our general variety simply don't like to be on their backs, and that goes for dragonesses, even though it is imperative that they, well, I mean, it's really the only possible way it can be managed on land. In short, they are simply exhausting to deal with, and this is partly why dragons have not increased appreciably, what with the *Wyrd,* the way we've had to spread out to these various outposts all over the world, and the nature of dragonesses.

This isn't to say, though, that we aren't attracted to dragonesses. We are mad about them. There's nothing like a really long squirm with a dragoness, preferably in a mellow tarn at eventide with the moon up, when it is possible to float in the water, where she doesn't kick as much, and to muffle the stifling smoke of her passion a bit—a really cool experience, those kids on the rock would call it—but only twice a year or so through the centuries, because it leaves you a bit damp, going on as it does for at least forty-eight hours, and then tired and very crocodile-sluggish in times when vigilance is the main, the only thing.

Well, the human beings on the rock. Yes, I'll admit I had to clear my throat because I was quite taken with this young chick, who looked as if she really, well, as if she really had it, as if she was someone I could reach out to and say, "Look, I'd like to be your dragon," or something as inane as all that, that's how she made me feel—in spite of my *Geis*. Because when she looked up in the trees for the mockingbird it seemed as if that song was just the most important thing in her whole life and that she adored it, she had given herself completely to that song, worshiped it. I had the feeling, unfortunately, that I could make her look at me that way. And then there was the whole thing I have been feeling so profoundly, that there is little time, that the human poet is right, that somehow, some way, *they must come to know.*

So I didn't even slither away. Besides, all thirty-two feet, six and a half inches of me was now not simply coiled in the shadowy darkness but sparkling in the waning light, for I could not resist displaying the best parts of me in the kind of light that is most flattering. The line of pointed triangles from my neck to the tip of my tail takes on a coloration like mother-of-pearl in such light. I know it does something to them. It is almost hypnotic. (I realize this preening is disgusting to some species, but we dragons are after all aesthetes, aesthetes of our own bodies, bejeweled, rainbowed in the moonlight—to say nothing of our capacities for fireworks.)

There I was, letting it all hang out, so to speak, or so she would no doubt speak; and Beautiful, who turns out to be named Bobby or some such inanity, lets it all out, too, in the form of a big Texas whoop and acrobatic leap, pulling my lovely girl-princess by the arm and saying it's time they got out of here, and she resisting, saying very calmly and in a rather matter-of-fact way, "It's only a dragon, Bobby."

"Only, for Chrissakes. Whaddya want before we take cover, Ronald Reagan breathing down on us? Come on." So, leaving his Nazi cap on the rock, he tries to drag her off toward the old dirt mountain road above, where now I see a big Yamaha motorcycle, staring Cyclops-eyed down on all the tragic scene. She goes reluctantly, looking back all the time, and I foolishly and unaccountably puff a smoke-ball semaphore. But how unaccountably? I suppose that our guarding has always really been an expression of love. I do out "L-O-V-E" in Morse code. She doesn't understand, I guess, but she must know IT'S SOME KIND OF MESSAGE. "So long, dragon," she says, as Bobby Beautiful varoom-varooms his Yamaha, skids the dust and leaves his semaphore for me. I'm angry. I shoot a ball of fire up at the dust, drive it away.

Foolish indeed. I could have caused a brush fire.

I sit there, if you can say dragons sit (this is the problem of using words designed for the human body). I . . .

haunch there, a bit stunned by this encounter and by my
own actions. First I wonder whether they will go back and
report me. I know this has been happening with the Sasquatch. They have not adjusted their habits to the camper
and hunter explosion. Too many teenagers and deputy
sheriffs up in the Northwest come upon them at night
when they have been out on their strolls. Even snapshots
taken, some claim. Gentle, friendly animals, they will be
hunted now. But, of course, in the larger picture they are
less important than we. It is their example the human
being will destroy when he destroys the last Sasquatch, the
example of their moral life, their spiritual gifts, their gen-
tility and courtierlike demeanor. With us more is at stake.
It is what we keep from human beings that makes our sur-
vival imperative.

Then I think, no, the two of them couldn't convince
anyone of my reality. Not those two, not Beautiful on his
chromium horse, not my sweetheart straddling it behind
him. Freaked out, high on drugs, they'd all say, no doubt.
So I go on, bearing my Chalice through the great crowd of
Oaks, who do not speak, though they are watching me. Re-
sentful of man, they will never tell. I return late at night
by the same route—to gather up the beer can and Beautiful's Nazi hat, of course.

On the next evening I am compelled to visit the rock
again. I could not say no. I have visited the rock because
of her. I have coiled myself on the rock in beautiful con-
centric circles, and I have crossed my foreclaws and put
my head doglike upon them, gazing down toward the tarn
in a pose designed to suggest moody intensity. If someone
comes by the road he will surely see me—some hunter,
perhaps. It is dangerous to be here. I feel somehow that I

want to be seen. It has been a hard day, I rationalize.
Only the great chests, which will be a job, and the Greater
Chalice are left to transport. I have talked myself into this
foolish relaxation. I am waiting, in the lower reaches of my
mind, I know, for her to come back to this rock, to this
wilderness place, in evening, somewhat far from anywhere,
and alone. Perhaps I am losing my mind.

She did not come that evening. After a time the wind
blew up and the Oaks swayed and whispered. A chill settled on the tarn. The water rippled, turned gray, then
black. I remained there for some time. It flashed through,
no, it preyed upon my mind that one could imagine wish-
ing to be more than a dragon, or less. But this odd thought
came upon me only as a single fluttering among thousands
of true dragon feelings. I went back to the barrow, after a
long swim.

I worked diligently all through the day in the tunnels,
shoring up for the transport of the seven chests, which I
shall carry under the mountain and then into the daylight
for the dangerous and open miles toward the new hidden
barrow. It is cliffside, beyond a marshy gulch. It will be
my last California home. I have already connected the new
halls by tunnel to a quite adequate tarn. I have electrified
the whole intricate arrangement with wall lights and chandeliers. The Great Hall, larger than the tumulus at New-
grange in my distant childhood memory, I have been carv-
ing with the greatest care. On the walls I shall create my
greatest works of historical art. I shall depict the vast mi-
grations from the sea, the dragon wars, the Great Council,
the spreading of dragons to the ends of Earth, each to
guard his appointed realm. I shall depict in the last panels
my friends Feuerkugel and Nasha. In the earlier, there will

flourish the great Welsh dragon wizard Ceugant, who is *all*
—reality's needle's eye; the Knäckerune, sea hunter and
poet; his sons of the green flames, and Eterskel: the line of
the Firedrakes, among whom I am perhaps the last to be
chosen as a guard.

Yesterday and today I have watched the rock. Restless
in the night I have prowled among the Oaks. It has been
quiet and the mockingbird has sung only toward morning.
Often over the centuries I have strolled to the tarn before
dawn to drink from its cool water or to swim. It is there in
recent months I have occasionally met a large brown owl
who sits on the arm of a favorite Oak. We dragons have
little social intercourse with the smaller animals. They do
not speak, and their lives are very short, and thus their
point of view is different from ours. The owl and the mole,
however, each in his own way, do have something in common with us, and I enjoy both. The mole knows Earth and,
though blind, and in so many ways defenseless, understands Earth's presence. I have spoken to moles. Occasionally a mole falls into one of my tunnels and I must care for
it while it is stunned or badly frightened. They do not
speak, but I believe they understand something of what I
try to say to them. They are fundamentally listeners, scholars if you will, of the true underworld.

This owl whom I have come to know is a most interesting person. Other creatures fear him, or attack him if
they are in superior numbers. He is an enemy of the moles
and other rodents. There is a viciousness in him, as there is
in other carnivores. But he understands us, even though he
is always guarded and, of course, suspicious of my friend-
ship with moles. He understands because he leads a lonely
and austere life. He too has been mythologized and possi-

bly maligned. He is the Halloween bird, an evil omen. There is, of course, something naturally chilling about his nocturnal appearance that brings out this response even in me, but I reject it. The owl in the tree, silent and staring in the dusk or darkness, seems better suited to representing the isolate mind. Perhaps he, too, guards mysteries, less definable than our own.

This early morning I stood below his tree and he swiveled his head around toward me. It is a feat he performs with a grace much to be admired. We stared at one another for some time. We have developed a way of communicating that is rather primitive, but successful within bounds. He cannot query me; I must anticipate his interests. If I have not done so he signifies my irrelevance by swiveling his head around so that he is no longer facing me. On the other hand, if I query him he answers in the affirmative by staring directly into my eyes. When he wishes to answer in the negative he flies off, and the conversation is effectively closed. There is a sort of game in it. If I wish to prolong the discussion I must frame questions so that an affirmative answer is forthcoming. No matter what sort of question, a negative answer causes him to lose patience, as if wisdom were Yes and I had insulted him. I have recently thought of asking him about his role in things, as if somehow his might reinforce our own, but I have been waiting for the proper framing of the question to come to me. As I stared at him, again it did not come, and instead I put a number of questions to him about the owlish attitude toward smog. It exercised him greatly. When we got to the question of what might be done he fluttered off abruptly.

I strolled on to the tarn, stared at its murky blackness and imagined I saw foam accumulating among the lily pads. I returned finally to my barrow. Today I have not worked at the tunnels. I have not spoken with Feuerkugel or with Nasha. I have thought much about Ireland and Lough Corrib, and my father and mother. I have reviewed my life and the meaning of dragons.

By human reckoning 1364 is a long way back, ages ago; but not by dragon time, for at 608 I am what a human being would call middle-aged and with the memory of everything, dragonlike, nearly to birth. Photographic, our memories. We project the most detailed remembrances of our past upon a cavern wall, a cloud, the flowing mist from the sea. There is nothing that escapes us or that, by the same token, we can escape. Perhaps this is why we have learned restraint, some dignity, and insist on a certain fastidiousness of behavior in ourselves. Early in our youth we sense our *Wyrd* or, to employ an inadequate modern word, *oath*. How can I explain? Men take *oaths*, but dragons discover their *Wyrd* or simply come to live it.

The Irish landscape is right for a young dragon, and Lough Corrib and Lough Mask, though very shallow for dragon taste, had the advantage of size and were connected by an underground river navigable even for the largest adults. My childhood was quiet. We grazed at night near the shore but fed mostly on lake weeds and brown trout. They were in such abundance that the monks at Cong merely dropped a line through the floor of their fishing house and read breviaries while they waited for the bite. Now and then one of us in the murky depths would yank the line and clean off the bait, just to perpetuate the story of huge creatures in the Lough. Overland at night we would stroll through the alternating fog, rain, mist, and clear, bracing air. There was little need for stealth in those days. The monks at the Abbey where Ireland's last high king had retired to live out his days were gentle people. The countryside was not much inhabited, and we were seldom worried when we came upon a lone human being or two lovers on the roads at night. There were stories of us among the people, but no attempt to rationalize us away as moralistic allegories or huge snakes. Every human being knew that St. Patrick had driven out the snakes centuries before, and when the young people went back to their cottages to say they had seen a dragon, their report was accepted. No electronic equipment scanned the Lough trying to prove or disprove that we were huge sea worms left over from the glacial melt. We were simply dragons.

In short, there was not much confusion around Cong at all until a young Brigit fell enamored of my younger brother Killaraus and then in a fit of defensiveness, when her parents upbraided her for staying out too late, claimed he had held her captive in a cavern for two days. The father was angry enough, and brave enough, to borrow a big old sword at the Abbey and come out to the Lough, where Dad calmed him with a couple of fireblasts across his bow; and then they sat down and discussed the whole thing like gentlemen over some very fine mead that Dad just happened to have brought up from the barrow. As a brewer of mead Dad was at least as competent as the monks.

It was a good relationship we had with the people when they came across us and were brave enough to stand their ground and not simply run away suddenly, as most of them did. And all that business of the dragon who said, "If the king's daughter is not here tomorrow at this same hour the realm shall be ravaged by me" (which is the way the Celtic dragon myth goes), is a creation of some young lady who simply wanted to get coiled up with one of us. It's merely sensationalism, like the stories human beings would tell of the trolls coming to get them. It is interesting how human beings like to scare the hell out of themselves.

There was one thing the old red-headed father didn't like about his conversation with Dad, though, and that was when Dad remarked that human girls had always really liked, I mean, really lusted after dragons. Old O'Cairbry screwed himself up pretty tight at that, and being a bit drunk with the mead he was ready to get back to protecting the honor of his daughter and all Irish womanhood. You could see that it wasn't really honor that was bothering him, but his own vanity. I saw his wife once, a fine lump of a girl indeed she was, and the young men half her age would watch her—as I did behind a hedgerow one day. The daughter favored her mother's dark, winsome face and hair, and the truth was that Killaraus might have ravaged all of Connaught to keep her if it wasn't becoming *Geis* for him to see her at all. He was soon to begin training for the Denmark post. There was very strict *Geis*, which is the other side of *Wyrd*, about human consorts during training and at any time thereafter. Dad wasn't trying to make any big braggarty drunken claims about dragon-appeal before O'Cairbry. That's not really in dragon character. He was just trying to explain to the actor himself the circumstances that had brought O'Cairbry out with his rusty sword. On the other hand, I always suspected that Dad enjoyed his verbal rapier thrust. Dad had the dragonistic habit of patience with human beings, but in the end he knew who was superior and he couldn't help expressing his real thoughts.

Years later, apparently, O'Cairbry tried to tell someone

in a pub at Cong that he'd talked with a dragon, bedad, and it didn't wash. It was all right among human beings to *see* a dragon; it was acceptable to be scared out of one's wits by one; but even the "degenerate Irish" (as the Normans came to call them) wouldn't believe that a dragon would sit down and carry on a socio-psychological conversation with a man. (Personally, I never cared much for the Normans and their stone towers and crude, haughty ways. We were Welsh in origin ourselves and related, as they say, better to the Celts. They knew these islands in their hearts.)

In short, there were no human forays against dragons in Ireland. The Irish dragon-slaying myth has no basis in fact and is of fairly recent date. It is a matter of national pride to construct such tales. I hardly even resent it, for it is a worldwide human compulsion—as collecting is a dragonish compulsion.

So Ireland was a good place in which to grow up—a nice climate, what with the precipitation. We don't mind the hot weather a bit, but the dryness does take something out of our hides. We like to remain slightly moist, and we don't want to be dusting and polishing our jewels all the time, which is the case here, especially with the real-estate developments and all the scarring and stupid squaring of Earth. But Old Earth will have His revenge when He speaks, or when in the nightmare of His torture by human surgeons He tosses and turns.

I am astonished at all the books I run across in my scavenging that try to define human purpose. It is a whole industry. With us purpose is perfectly clear, and the great spoken texts, mainly the *Great Blerwm* of Knäckerune in twelve books, reach always the same ethical conclusion.

My childhood was devoted in part to the learning of this lore, the assignment of my role in the prophecy, my training for the role, and finally the bestowal of responsibility upon me. There were others of my generation, of course, undergoing a similar education, suited to the particular wilds to which they would be dispatched: Manlyr, given the difficult task of setting right the false mythology of plumed dragons in the South. Feuerkugel and Nasha to the North. Killaraus, dispatched to the supposed scenes of Beowulf's triumph—all of us under the ultimate tutelage of the latest in the line of the great Ceugants in Lin Ligua, deep in the Welsh highlands of Radnorshire. By which meridian all dragons set the clocks of their becoming.

The training began when I was fifty. Until the young dragon reaches that age it is not practical to do more than put in his mind the twenty-eight metrical and alliterative patterns of dragon lore, invented, it is said, by the deity Annwn (whom Welshmen stole for their own) and exploited each through their twelve hundred variations by Knäckerune in the twelve books. We learned these from our mothers line by line. Then there came for each of us the trial of the eight rhythms—that is, the creation of poems in each of these styles and exposure to the ruthless criticism of our peers once weekly in the dreaded workshops of Cainudy, Oaklun, Galwei, and (most awful) of Mihalmac, student in ages past of the great Yvordrake, who smoked codes of disgust at the sky should any student falter in his syllabic count. All this was of the spirit. The flame and smoke of our mentors awed us, for until about age sixty-five the young dragon is fireless. Our mothers and their simpler alliterative lessons came to seem like the caresses of Eden in the face of Mihalmac, but we followed on, and not one of us failed to master the lore, not one of us has forgotten.

Aside from performing these exercises of the mind we became impertinent tricksters, cunning fishermen, implacable though mysterious foes of the dam builders and other occasional defacers of the lakes and streams.

We dragons remember so much that we are not quite capable of human nostalgia, but should we be capable, my croco— my dragon tears would be shed over the days in Lough Corrib, the race through the underground river to Lough Mask. Years ago I composed some lines on it in humanoid verse, having picked up an old Wordsworth one evening after people had deserted a rummage sale. I liked best those lines about his youth. Wordsworth had a dragon's soul, as we say. It is almost impossible for me, given my education, not to try my hand at any style I come across. Here I return to the evening in which I discovered, for the first time, the connecting stream to Lough Mask:

That autumn evening nosing out I sought
The northern edges of the glittering lake
My usual home, intent upon the tale
Our father rimed deep in the rocky lair.
The human boats stood still upon the lake,
The rising moon rippled the lake to gold,
But all along the edge the silence ruled.
Finning forth I chose my lone smooth way
Leaving a trail of water like a swan,
And then dove far into the murky depths
Of Corrib's northern shore, therein to find
The rushing passage 'neath a craggy ridge.
I flowed like water, smooth as eels would swim,

Until my breath burst fire in the dark cave,
Rising in Mask to see that oval huge
Hang o'er the hills like Annwn's fearful eye,
Casting on me the oath that I
Would follow back to Corrib and beyond.
In afterdays, floating upon my mind,
This orb with Annwn's word combined to claim
Upon me *Wyrd* and *Geis* not to return
Without my promise kept, the Hoard retained.

Alliteration and rhyme creep in, because that's *our* style.

The physical training follows. It is the dangerous part because a young dragon is possessed of powers that can be a torment to himself and the whole neighborhood if he does not learn to control them. It is the constant threat of conflagration that presents the greatest problem. A young dragon, in the most difficult time of his life, which is without question ignitiety, is inclined to belch flame in his sleep, or at the worst to smoke up the lair. This is one of the reasons for tarns, wherein a young dragon can plunge himself, if necessary. These things the stripling must learn to control. Exercise is a help, and dragonschool emphasizes strenuous activity for at least half the day. Indeed, it is necessary. Though there is a bit of lizardlike sloth in us, which sends us against our better judgment sunning on rocks in the afternoons, we are soon convinced that our *Wyrd* (its precise details only growing upon us) will require the most perfect conditioning.

Those were active days. I remember them with the pleasure that goes with accomplishment. Even the unpleasant moments I now recognize as necessary, though I naturally prevent them from metamorphosing into a cloud of sentiment.The first long stealthy trip overland was frightening, so much seemed at stake. I traveled north to Killala Bay, charged with securing a relic from Moyne Abbey. It was my hundredth year, a strong young dragon I was, of length twenty-six feet at the stretch, but of my trip I knew almost nothing. It is always so designed. The Abbey was new, only four years old; I had been told of the tower that commanded a view all around. A simple chalice, a breviary, an illuminated manuscript, or some lesser object of clothing—this was the sort of thing I must secure and bring safely back to Corrib, together with a complete report of the countryside, the people observed, including an account of any meetings I might have with man or beast. The fewer of these the better. Honor system, of course. It was never clear at that time just why we should bring something back, and with the idea of *any*thing a certain irrelevance seemed to enter our education. But now I see that there was a challenge in it. The hidden test was to obtain something not necessarily of human value but symbolic of one's own daring and bravery. This was also our first training in disciplining the dragon compulsion to collect.

It was late afternoon when I first saw the Abbey tower. I was soon to know the goal of my quest. The good monks were finishing its construction, but in their own Celtic time—between tea breaks and hand-warming conversation around small fires. They had hoisted a fine wrought-iron vane to the tower top, and I recognized its symbol as—the likeness of a dragon! Lying behind a wall of piled stone, peering through the tangled brambles, I plotted how it could be mine. I would have to scale the outer walls. Any approach through the interior would surely be noticed. In that beautifully clear air, on that night of sailing moon and clouds, I climbed as I had never climbed before, holding to windows and ledges like a gigantic chameleon on a wall, until I reached the top. Then, coiling myself completely around the tower, I paused. The sky was momentarily clear and the moon came through and lit the sandy island, across which I saw for the first time in my life the great expanse of the sea. I cannot express how this experience moved me, for in its sudden glittering there came before me the meaning of those stories my mother had told me—the creation myths of our race, that date from before the *Great Blerwm*. I knew that my ancestors had voyaged upon, indeed commanded, the seas, that we were Aquarians all, and that my cousins, the Blue Nicors, still frolicked there. It was our *Wyrd* in the age of man to do our important work upon the land, from our barrows, hollowed halls, and deep tarns.

Struck dumb, I stared at the sea and recognized the inevitability of my own quest, which I knew—as if Ceugant had been whispering it, complete with alliteration, into my ear—must take me over the great Atlantic to the hills where I now abide. When my attention came back to the business of my trophy, I saw that the dragon of the vane was not the classic dragon I had thought it, but the imagining of some mist-crazed blacksmith-monk. It was a great whale-beast—Job's Leviathan, deepest of demons. It predicted my sea voyage.

I was but a moment fire-breathing it to sever it from its base, *mon semblable, mon frère.*

From these quests and various trials we are put to in our youth come the stories of dragons ravaging the countryside, killing everything in sight, and demanding young maidens, or fighting knights. Lies, all lies! Or inaccuracies. Petty theft, only.

My quest was a success, and I was much applauded for the quality of my trophy, the symbolic value of which was certainly not lost on my elders, for (as I had intuited, in the way we dragons intuit all principles of the most abstruse geometries) the trophy predicts the quest. Knäcke-rune has written cryptically:

> Search then the unknown:
> short is one's stay
> once the great prophet
> proffers the image.

Everything after that was a foregone conclusion, though the exact order, the formal bestowal, never came as an explanation, only as a wordless confirmation of what I had come to be prophet of—myself.

I was well trained for endurance. I accomplished the run to Iceland, slipping into Galway Bay, voyaging north of the Arans past treacherous Rockal to Vestmannaeyjar's smooth inlet at Heimaey, and thence across water to climb Eyjafjallajökull's fifty-five hundred feet, chosen over Hekla for its greater height.

In spite of my experience with the North Atlantic, the appointed journey itself was not easy. No one had ever said it would be. For a time it appeared that I should remain longer in Corrib or be farmed to some other Lough in the Isles, as was Gowra to Loch Ness. The sixteen Hoards over the globe, eight each in the Eastern and Western Leagues, as they were called, were presided over by competent and experienced workers with deep fires in their breasts. No retirements were contemplated among those to whose replacement my prophecy could conceivably refer. What the solution to this problem might be I did not know. The years that next passed were busy enough with the waiting, however. I kept to a rigid round of exercise and studied human history. I was eventually betrothed and united to a young dragoness from the Welsh tarn, Gwynfyd Ab Bleher, and we awaited the birth of our first child. There was a lot of the Celtic highland in Gwynfyd. She was a restless beast, active and athletic, long, silky of tail, and the best match I have met at the game of quarles.

Then came the great assembly of the Presidium, centered at Lin Ligua, where it was acknowledged by all that the time for expansion had come. There were four new Hoards needing protection in the West. It was the changing human character of the American continents that brought into being and required measures to protect these western Hoards, made from man's desire and from his greed—man, who seemed unable to create his own prophecies and live them out. And so the Western League was expanded to ten and then twelve, and the stock of young, capable dragons without major Hoards diminished by four. In the East, too, the Hoards increased equally. Everywhere that man gained technical knowledge or began to mine or devastate Earth, there identical Hoards came into being; to those places dragons were dispatched; there dragons dug.

I set forth. The salt sea to the South held many creatures I had not seen before. I swam for days toward the Isthmus of Panama, where I would take to the land, following roughly the trail covered now by the great canal. The voyage was tiring but uneventful. To cross now as

I did then would be unthinkable. I swam the surface directly to the Azores, caught the current of the trade winds, passed through the area of brown sargossa weed, voyaged just south of what is now called Puerto Rico, and on to Panama. In all of that time and space I saw but two ships, and my presence was known to neither. Small sailing craft they were by today's standards, and moving slowly with excess of cargo. It was 1564, my two-hundredth year.

I came ashore where Santa Barbara now is and where the land juts out so that the sea is to the South. I had been observed by no one but a few whales, perhaps, some sharks who showed me absolute respect, and two Blue Nicors I had met off the Azores. Happy and carefree, my cousins the Nicors. Fireless and without our instinct, they were simpler than we, trivial in their occupations and wants. Double-finned, unbejeweled, they had never found the land hospitable, had been content with the sea. In truth, we looked down upon them, as we looked down upon the White Nicors, their enemies, who sank long ago into the ocean depths. The Blue Nicors are not offended by our attitudes, and these two played like dolphins about me as I swam, laughing and talking a sort of amiable nonsense. They referred to the Atlantic as "their ocean" in a paternalistic sort of way that was still possible to them before man began filling it with ships, then with the refuse of his civilization, then fighting over it as if it were his to pick up and carry home.

I was none too early. The Spaniards were well on their way to dominating the Indian tribes that had lived here peacefully and without despoiling the land for centuries. The Spaniards' ambition, and later the surge of Americans westward across the plains, had made Ceugant's decision

to expand the Western League inevitable. He had foreseen
the necessity of sending guards to the western Hoards.
There must always be, for man, something that he seeks but
does not find.

So I located the Hoard in the hills beyond the coast,
and it became my trust, as the wordless prophecy had fore-
told. I had left Gwynfyd and our dragonchild in Ireland,
as all the other nineteen Hoard-keepers had left their
mates and children, who would soon embark on their education. Hoardolatry, one of the Blue Nicors had laughingly
called it. I had been amused. Of course.

The making of the original network of tunnels and the
halls took a hundred years. And now I am moving everything, buying the rest of the time that we and man shall
need. Ceugant was not pleased with my original choice of
site. I had thought it more convenient as a base for collecting than one farther inland, and it had a superb tarn.
Wiser than I, Ceugant foresaw the rape of the coastland by
man.

March 17

For two evenings I have emerged in late afternoon following work in the tunnels, and I have gone to the rock.
The air has been clear, the breeze from the Southwest. I
have listened quietly. It is my sense that some human
being is nearby. Is it wishful thinking? Am I being
watched? Is there danger to the Hoard?

March 19

Near the rock I was when yesterday I became certain of that presence above me near the old road. I stiffened, tail straight, holding a deep breath in the cauldrons of my firelungs. I would do nothing until whoever it was made some gesture. Earth-despoiler, perhaps. A lost hiker. She? I waited. Silence.

It must have taken all her courage; she came hesitantly from behind thick bushes, dressed as she had been before, in jeans and shirt. She stopped perhaps twenty yards from me, held out her hand, palm up. I was amused, and touched by this; she wished to be friends. I relaxed my tail, released my firehoard in nostril smoke, puffing again my futile code. She was startled. I twitched the end of my tail slowly, catlike, waved it in the air. She smiled hesitantly.

"Hello, dragon," she said. Her voice was thin, a bit hoarse. "Hello."

Should I speak? I had spoken to only a few human beings in centuries. I was self-conscious, worried about the reaction my voice would elicit. After all, it has been a matter of faith with them that only they have the gift of words. Her approach had been friendly, but it was the friendliness of the child with the dumb animal. I hesitated. Would she say anything more?

"Hello, dragon, nice dragon." She would come no closer until I did something. Physical movement—all the nuances of the body known to dragons—would only startle her. She could not afford to trust me without words. I wanted to speak, of course, but I was uncertain how to proceed. Would my voice sound gross and uncouth to her? Should I maintain a discreet formality, a suave worldliness? My mind raced through all the forms of greeting in my dragon experience, but they seemed unsuitable. And so I bowed my head, arching my neck with as much grace and dignified courtliness as I could summon, remembering my father when Ceugant presented to him my betrothed.

"I am glad you came," I said, head still bowed in greeting. I had meant to say that she shouldn't be afraid. I gasped more air; some smoke puffed out. I found that I was quite nervous. She smiled, still hesitant. Then I said, "Don't be afraid. I shan't harm you."

"But you could."

"Yes, of course, but I shan't."

"You may not wish to be bothered. I mean, do you want to be alone? You gave us a real fright the other day."

"Then why did you return?"

She was silent, bowed her head, looked up slowly through her great, and I thought genuine, eyelashes. "I—I don't know . . . I—I—well, you know, like I guess I wanted to—to know . . ." and she couldn't go on.

"But didn't you think it would be dangerous? After all, you must have heard stories about dragons, the myths, the legends," and then I began to wonder whether it wasn't the generation gap I was facing. Were these kids ever really scared, I mean *really* scared by anything, what with Kukla, Fran, and Ollie, the Friendly Dragon, the disgusting dragons of Disney with their stupid sentimentalism, and the countless cuddly stuffed dragons anyone could buy at White Front, Sav-On, and the department stores? Why, even Dracula and Frankenstein—the whole generation must think of them as freaky comedies. It made me feel old and useless, a huge, lumbering, oil-smoking Pierce-Arrow hunted down mercilessly by a mob of Volkswagens, laughing and impertinent. For a second I wanted to lower the curtains on my windows all around, to say go away. But it wasn't that simple.

"I didn't believe in them, I mean you, I—I mean, well, I didn't think they were, you know, real, really real; then, I saw you up here that day with—I mean, when I was with Bobby—and you didn't look . . . well, you were—were *interesting*." She hadn't moved any closer to me, just stood there. I had the feeling that she would stand there forever if I didn't do something. But I couldn't very well say something like "Come closer, my dear," without sounding as if I'd stepped out of *Little Red Riding Hood*. Besides— "interesting," I thought. A strange attitude, new in the best modern way, a far cry from the pretty Spanish girl, and so far from what I'd learned about human women in Ireland that I almost laughed at it or at myself. I guessed that she'd want to touch the jewels along my back. The great dragon theorist Brontasauri had laid out the principles of see-and-touch eons ago from the Center for Dragon Culture at Como. Human beings had adopted her mode of pythonetics only in this century. It was bearing results, I could see, perhaps good ones, though I had the distinct feeling that the old dragon graces of courtliness kept dragons from too headlong flight, while human beings would plunge ever ahead.

Well, I'd be "interesting," if that was the right role. I was up on roles and games people play. A dragon can always come by a best seller tossed in a garbage heap. And very interesting I was, too, come to think of it. In addition to my firemaking and smoke-signaling, which were cheap tricks at best, I could be a walking history of Western, mostly Celtic man, a chronicler of the sea, a geologist, an expert on valuable antiques and jewelry, and a scholar with the power to correct the numerous errors of Frazer, Weston, Freud, Jung, and the whole psychoanalytic and comparatist school when it came to dragons, worms, and phallic beasts in general.

The truth was, though, that I was quite foolishly, considering dragon *Geis*, taken by this young thing about ten yards away from me, and I was preening myself, polishing my great jeweled back before the mirror of my mind. I didn't want to be just interesting, I wanted to be *fascinating*.

Pleased with myself, glorying in my self-satisfaction, I gallantly proposed that we sit on a rock and talk. She seemed hesitant. I think she wondered whether I had effective control of my fires, whether perhaps I might burn her up by mistake. Maybe that was because she knew that she had struck a spark in me, if you will pardon the expression. And so we proceeded to the rock. I would have preferred a real walk, but it is absolutely impossible for a human being and a dragon to walk together comfortably for any distance. We cover ground much faster than they. While the human being beside us is practically sprinting along, we must move in fits and starts. As a result it always ends up that they want to *ride* us. Maybe it's because they can't give up thinking of us as domesticable animals, or maybe it's just for the fun of it. This happened to Killaraus with the O'Cairbry girl. He didn't mind being ridden once or twice, he said, but there's no doubt that it changed their

relationship, if ever so slightly. He got tired of being ca-
joled and begged for a ride and then, I guess, became bitter and even said to her one day that all she really wanted
was a goddamned horse, and then she cried, and then he
relented and became a goddamned horse.

Anyway, now it's too dangerous to go on walks in the
daytime, because of the possibility that the real-estate people will that day finally advance to these hills and come
upon us, or us upon them.

So, as I said, we did not take a walk, merely proceeded a few yards to the rock. I coiled on it, and she
perched, knees up, chin on knees, facing me. She was con-
templating me. She was appreciative. I'll say that much.

"Can dragons smile?" she asked.

"We can if we work at it. It isn't natural." Knäckerune's seventeenth warning from the *Great Blerwm* naturally came to my mind:

> Fallow the dragon face,
> Eyes are their exits.
> Humans would harrow in
> Soft cymric sentiment.

He goes on, but the point is that the human being requires
facial contortion as a help to communication. We dilate
our eyes, change their color to express feeling, and that
suffices us. I explained this, then said that, yes, I could
smile, but she might think it frightening, even unpleasant.

But then I learned something about human beings, for
her eyes lit up. They actually changed. And she just
looked right into me, right down into this old wyrm with
her eyes, which were big and brown, and which I wished
she hadn't made owlish with all that mascara or whatever
it was women in hordes had been putting around their

eyes for about ten years now. And she said, "Oh please, do smile, do."

Knäckerune was no doubt trying to warn dragons through all time that it didn't make sense for dragons to smile, that it led to misunderstanding. Human beings tended to think a smile either an invitation to excessive intimacy or a false geniality. Either way you couldn't win. Nevertheless, I had learned to smile those centuries before, practicing furtively before a glassy tarn for the girl from Santa Barbara. But I never actually smiled at her. The *Great Blerwm* warned against it.

Now I threw caution to the wind and tried to capture this acquired and then lost art. First, however, I explained how it had been a long time, and on this first effort I wouldn't smile in her direction for fear of unintentionally igniting my breath or smoking through my nostrils. I made a bad joke about violating the anti–air-pollution law, and *she* smiled a really great smile that shivered my triangles, and then *I* smiled.

It came slowly, involving first a display of the six frontal teeth that nestle between our two sets of huge upper and lower fangs. If this was all, it would probably not be so frightening, but once embarked on a display of these teeth in what would amount only to a slightly broken smirk, the dragon cannot stop. He must proceed to reveal the massive side teeth, the green gums, and of course the great golden tongue, which inevitably protrudes its two forks. There is NOTHING the dragon can do about this protruding of the tongue when he attempts a human smile. It is a reflex. He cannot even grimace with his mouth closed. All those shows of emotion must be done with the eyes. It is either this awful guffaw of a smile or eyeplay.

She was delighted. I thought, Oh my God, she'll be

getting me to do it all the time now, and she'll be riding me next. She was delighted, because she didn't just smile some more, she laughed, she threw back her head and laughed. For a moment I was embarrassed, afraid she had thought me ridiculous, but then I felt rising inside of me a tremendous rush of absurd frivolity. In my cauldrons the air seethed and burned. I raised my head to the heavens and roared in mirth a huge fireball and black smoke. I had laughed, too. I turned my eyes a deep blue.

It was a startling display, and I did not blame her for jumping a bit. Watching the smoke billow up out over the trees in the wind, she said, "Say, that was something!" And I was certain she'd want me to do it again, but she didn't say so, just put her head back on her knees and stared at me as if I were simply the most marvelous thing she had ever seen, which no doubt I was.

March 20

I have not told all of what we did or said two days ago after my great laughter. For a while the two of us were silent, she watching me, and I now wary of her eyes. Where did we go from there? I recognized the uniqueness of my stunning appearance, but I knew, too, that in some way I must be unreal to her—romance come to life, a creature to be observed and marveled upon as if he were a work of human art, almost a literary convention, meaning false or historically untrue. That is an uncomfortable position, a role that demands a huge expenditure of restraint from a dragon, whose own myths are always history. Worse, it does not enable one to *do* anything, for the traditional and, of course, false dragon role in human myth is that of awful miserly ferociousness. The mythic dragon's activities are limited pretty much to guarding and increasing Hoards of material gold, despoiling the countryside, and carrying off maidens.

It is true that we will fight when challenged. It is true that we guard treasures. But never have we despoiled the countryside to gain a personal advantage, or to increase the treasure, nor have we carried off maidens. As I say this I know you are thinking about the dragon carrying off Krinhild and stories of that ilk. Dragon history records no such events. There have been affairs, yes, but only between Hoardless dragons and consenting human beings. I swear it. Nor are we prepared, even before a fascinated audience such as I now possessed, to act as if we ever could have done such things. It is *Geis;* it is, I have always thought, against our nature.

The only possibilities for me, then, would be either to behave in a most dignified and stylish way, as dragons are wont to do, or to descend into the depths of the human sentimentalized version of the dragon. Friendly old Puff or dreadful Pufnstuf. That would mean dragonback rides, more fireballs in the sky, foolish tail-waving, rolling on one's back, and ultimately all loss of self-respect. Terribly dangerous for a dragon, who just might despoil a country-side or two once he came to his senses and recognized the depths of his ignominy. I can't think of a case in which this has happened to a mature Hoarding dragon, because we dragons are fundamentally self-composed, even in adversity.

But how does one remain self-composed while one is

being stared at and admired all through a tête-à-tête? Not addressed, but simply observed, a dragon can usually remain aloof or preoccupied; he does not, like a dog, always have to invent a flea or clean his paws. Besides, I sensed that behind all of her admiration there was a sort of knowing impertinence.

I relaxed my tail and rearranged it in an excellent coil around the rock. Perhaps I executed this maneuver with more flourish and gratuitous sinuous waving than was absolutely necessary. Her eyes glowed. She was delighted. She said, "Groovy."

It recomposed me at once and made me regret my exhibitionistic lapse, for I hate that human word. I suppose it's the disk jockeys I hear. I turned slowly toward her and stared, coolly green-eyed and definitely haughty, then modulated my eyes to a lemon yellow.

"Wow."

She was observant, or tuned in, as they say, and didn't miss a nuance of my color scheme.

"I mean, you're a regular light show." And I saw that I'd have to control my eyes, not display them, because she would reduce me to carnival proportions. The whole set of assumptions I made about my eyes she and her world probably didn't any longer share. What could a dragon's eyes do these days against whole environments of light and all of human electronics?

It was a despairing moment. I visualized my eyes from her point of view: a huge color projector, attached to a computer. But then as I stared at her, my eyes became orange; and then they changed to a soft brown, for I watched hers fill and overflow ever so slightly with tears. Was she moved by this mechanical monstrosity before her?

Was it possible that the human imagination could draw real sentiment through the filter of a mechanistic view of all living things? But she *had* been moved.

"Those colors all *mean* something, don't they?" she said, her eyes brimming. "That's something. I mean, I hadn't thought; I—why, they *mean* something, and yet I—I can't really ask you what they mean, like each of them, I mean. You know, it would be impossible to say exactly, wouldn't it?"

"Yes." At least the way she was going, like.

"I mean, it's like they mean themselves, and it's the way they change, you know, and blend from one to another, and . . ."

"Yes, indeed, that is correct."

"But, well, I suppose you can *do* a color, or does it just happen?"

I did not want to answer the question, because no matter what the answer——

But I knew I must. "Yes, we can control our color, but there are times when we do not, when we don't consciously control it, but that is rare among us, I should say, after age one hundred or so."

"Gosh." It was the age that got to her, and I had hoped it would; and when you consider it's only about a tenth of a healthy dragon's life, given a good tarn nearby. . . . Always impressive. But she persisted, after a moment's quiet.

"If you control it, I mean, if you can just like turn on, I mean, turn on any color, why then it's not really sincere, is it? I mean, it's all controlled, and I can't read you. I ought to ignore it, because you'd—well, you know, you'd be *controlling* it."

It was inevitable that this would happen. It is a matter

that is very difficult to explain satisfactorily to a human being. Should I begin by discussing these false distinctions in a largely human philosophical framework, with all the terminological difficulties, or should I resort to the relevant lines in the Standard English translation of the *Great Blerwm?* Neither would do. I was impatient and did not wish to seem pedantic. I would have to say:

"It isn't that way with dragons. We think about how we should act, what role we should play, but we always end up playing ourselves. That is, we are sincere, because we don't make the old distinction between feeling and acting, feeling and rationality, or . . ."

"You've gotten rid of the *dichotomy*, gee."

Well, I had gone to great lengths to avoid the word. Bravely, now, I proceeded: "I don't mean that quite, either. We run into problems of decisions to be made, choices, of course, but we're . . ." I had almost said we were under oath, but that wasn't quite right, because I wasn't sure she'd understand what an oath was in our sense of *Wyrd* and *Geis*. In fact, as I've said, "oath" isn't a good word. We hadn't all been lined up before the pennant of that greatest of wyrms, Ceugant, and told to raise up our claws and repeat after me. Dragons never put things down in that way. Nor would it be proper to say that we were fated, or that we were mere automatons, programmed at birth. We all had *chosen*, and no dragon, since the primal times sung by Knäckerune, when Ercllyr descended with the other White Nicors into the Atlantic depths (there to plot an ultimate revenge), has forsaken that unspoken choice. "It's just that, well, we are what we are. And things are as they are." Besides, to bring up the oath would be to reveal too much. These creatures had insatiable inquisitiveness to go along with their compulsion to discard, and that was the whole point, of course.

"Gee." She seemed perplexed for a moment. There were no longer any tears in her eyes, merely a single one glistening on her cheek. I wished to reach over and wipe it away, but I didn't, thinking she would be startled by a huge claw coming toward her, no matter how handsome it was, and how carefully groomed. She was looking off over the hills, inside herself. Then she smiled. "Yeah, gee, it's . . ."

"Interesting," I interrupted. I was afraid she'd say "groovy" again. She observed me quizzically.

"Yeah, interesting," she said.

Later, March 20

Soon I shall go out to the rock and wait for her visit. I keep thinking about the inappropriateness of it at this time, indeed the strangeness of it. I castigate myself: our relationship cannot be for anyone's good. There is too much for her to learn, and too much that I must keep from her. I have not worked as efficiently as I should have with the chests in the tunnels. Then I think again upon her, remembering that she said nothing for a while after I had tried to explain my eyes. She was preoccupied with what I had told her, withdrawn perhaps into her humanity, which is *other* than me. Soon we were talking about how she had come this way with her friend Bobby on the motorcycle. They weren't lost, really, just off the beaten path. She had wanted to go up into the hills, away from the club, the other riders, the highways, the noise and smog, to see the birds. She loved the birds. But Bobby had been bored, no, not bored, on edge, didn't really like all the trees and nothing but nature around. Funny, though. Sometimes he just wanted to get away too, but for him getting away was never stopping and watching anything, just driving on and on. On and on, she mused. And when the dragon came, well, Bobby didn't even see the birds sometimes, and he was still wondering, right now probably, whether he'd really seen the dragon. Or had she witched it up for him —she and the hallucinogens he'd been messing around with?

I had been worried about that. I didn't need a whole herd of human beings tramping through the woods searching the way it happened with the Sasquatch sightings. Not right at this time, certainly, and preferably at no time, but I couldn't tell her all about that, for it was part of my *Geis,* of course. I did try to check out whether Bobby had said much about the dragon, and the answer was a vague no. He'd said something about going off the stuff, she remembered. But the truth was, she'd sort of avoided seeing Bobby since it happened. Oh, they'd talked about it right afterwards, that is, he'd talked and she'd listened, he convinced now he'd just had a great vision, and with no help from acid or rope or anything except his own expanded mind. Like the windows of perception were flung wide open, she said. And she'd made no comment to him at all, because she knew she'd really seen a dragon, and hadn't just freaked out. After that she'd thought and thought about the dragon. She told me this as if she were talking about someone else, some other dragon, or that she'd forgotten I was the dragon in question. It was very odd. It was as if she wanted to believe in real dragons, not just mind-blowing visions. But it was more than that, too, though I wasn't sure just what more it was. She was puzzling to me, a *tabula rasa* in a way, just as her face had that appealing blankness of youth. Blank, yes, but with the potentiality of feeling or capacity for passion, too. It was strange.

So she had taken her Volkswagen over the rocky, bumpy, dusty road into the hills, and found the rock again, and waited. She had known, even as they ran in flight from me, that she would come back.

"So you weren't really frightened."

"Ha, why of course I was, utterly like spooked. Man, do you think I'm crazy or something? I mean, well, yes, I guess I am." And we sat there a little while longer, quietly, as Sun set and the sky darkened, and she said in a very matter-of-fact, almost cold way that puzzled me, considering the excitement she could express, "Well, I've been up here long enough. Gotta get back."

"Would you like to come again?"

"You inviting me? That's really cool. Think of being invited to the dragon's. Like, well, I mean Alice has nothing on me, has she? But, hey, I didn't need an invitation this time, did I?"

"No, you didn't." I neglected to mention my unread semaphore.

"Well, I'll come again. Yeah, maybe it would be fun. Day after tomorrow maybe."

"I'll be here," I said in a quietly dignified manner. And she jumped up and ran up the hill. She ran fast for a girl. At the top, on the road edge, she turned and waved and shouted, "Hey, dragon, where's your Hoard?" and then, laughing, she was gone.

Midnight, March 20

She confessed that she had been here twice before approaching me. She had been lurking behind rocks and trees. She had observed me swim in the tarn: "Hey, y'know you really play around in the water. And all the steam!" I admitted to frivolity. Perhaps the water brings out the Blue Nicor in us. And she had seen me choosing the most succulent grasses, leaves, and berries. I was really cool the way I sniffed and rejected all but the best, and what a *great* tongue! Strange, thinking back, I had sensed some presence, but had not investigated. I had been too preoccupied with getting the barrow prepared, working against time. Grazing, I had thought only on my work. I must remember to follow up these intuitions in the future, to be constantly on my guard. Yet it is more difficult to concentrate on the work, what with her visits and I thinking on her conversations.

Let me say that although my direct knowledge of human beings is limited, dragon theory on the subject reached a very high degree of sophistication during the human age of ancient Greece, and we have all studied the major texts. Clearly I am intrigued at making direct acquaintance with a human being after so many years. Puzzling creatures surely, if she is typical, and that is what I would like to know. Is she? I cannot imagine that she is. I keep reminding myself of the danger, as Ceugant warned, of coming to know them too well, of recognizing and accepting their faults, their limitations, until one is no longer sufficiently careful about the Hoard. Yet I indulge in fond hopes for her life, for a sort of fulfillment.

I am nervous. Her parting remark was a joke, I suppose, but how can one be sure? Does she really think that I am guarding something in these hills? Why is it that she has not asked more about me? Could she have seen more than she has let on? Oh, Annwn! Perhaps she really believes all those stories about dragons guarding treasures. That is the one thing man has managed to get right about us! And if she believes those stories, why, then, perhaps she is really interested in the Hoard and not, as my vanity supposes, in dragons, or specifically in me. But that is foolish. If she were interested in the Hoard, how could she possibly expect to capture it alone? Unless she is an agent.

Early, March 21

It is amazing that there have not been more human women carried off, for indeed we can feel lustful toward them, as I feel toward her whose name I do not even know. And perhaps that is why she has been sent, to disarm me and lead me to reveal the secrets. I am on my guard.

Later, March 21

Scene: We are sitting on a larger shaded rock farther from the road where she parks the Volkswagen. "I left Faith sitting under a tree up there where at least it's a bit cool," she remarks, chewing on a long piece of grass. I am startled for a moment until I realize she is referring to the Volkswagen. Then I laugh. It is her turn to be startled, though my flame is discreet. I say, "You mean it takes Faith to ride in a Volkswagen on those freeways."

"Yeah," she says. It is not one of her more endearing expressions. "My brother has one he calls 'Hope.'" With satisfaction she watches my smoke rise.

"No 'Charity'?"

"No, but there *was* a 'Welfare.' It was a Chrysler, though. My father cracked it up on the Santa Ana Freeway coming back from the Reagan celebration in 1966. Fred and I named it posthumously." I wonder whether I am now to receive a little homily on the generation gap. It does not come. Nothing comes. Near us, regardless of our huge and central presence, three wild daisies are growing. Deftly I reach down to pick one, sparing two. I present it to her gravely.

"Neat," she says, taking it. "Real neat."

I watch her. Good heavens, she is chewing on a petal, she is *eating* my flower! I gave her a flower and she ate it, petal by petal! I have watched her do this thing silently. There is nothing to say about it.

Finally I ask, "Why are you coming up here every day?"

"I dunno." She is chewing.

"Sure?"

"Yeah, it's just like I have this big lust for dragons. You know, Leda with swans, queens with unicorns. I just freak out over dragons. Say, like, can you fly with those wings? They don't look as if they could keep you up."

I appreciate her erudition, but I am a bit wounded by

the observation about my wings. A touchy subject with dragons, for it is nearly true. We are about as airworthy as chickens.

"No, can't fly much. I get off the ground if I take a run at it, and I could soar, I suppose, from a height, but the wings are really swimming fins. We're Aquarians, you know."

"Oh, I'm an Aries."

"I hadn't meant that." I have always felt contempt for human astrology, which like a number of other things is a corruption of dragon lore, never meant to be a system of prediction, but of poetic prophecy, in the ethical sense.

There is silence.

"Who knows why I do things? I don't know. Most of what I do I can't explain. Can you?"

"You mean, what *you* do?"

"No what *you* do. Like giving me the daisy." This remark bothers me. Why did I give her the daisy? What are my intentions? "Yeah, dragon, say, what *do* you do?" I am suspicious and probably look it. "I mean, do you just hang around up here, grazing or something? I mean, you aren't pillaging or guarding a treasure in some cave, you aren't a prince in disguise?"

"No, those are frogs." She smiles. I am still wary, but pretty certain by now of her innocence.

"That business of asking me why I came was a serious question, wasn't it? Well, I—I—I was, you know, curious. I sorta see you as a possible friend. I mean you seem to be, like, in control of things." Pause. Chewing the daisy stalk. She throws it away suddenly, then twirls several strands of black hair around her finger, chews the hair.

"You are chewing your hair."

"Yeah, I do that. I do lots of neurotic things like that. I don't suppose you dragons do those things."

"Why do you suppose that?"

"Well, I don't know. It's just like you don't *have* any hair to chew, or fingernails, or . . ." It is true that we don't suffer the indecisiveness of human beings. I elect not to enter upon a discussion of my collecting compulsion. Anyway, it can't be a neurosis when we all do it and always have.

"We like to roll in the dust and shake. Some of us have a thing about polishing our back jewels, but that's a kind of fastidiousness or . . ."

"Narcissism."

Is education a good thing, I wonder. "Yes, well, we dragons do sneak a look at ourselves in the tarn now and then."

"Gee, that's groovy, I mean you talk just like myth and ritual. Like do you really talk that way about tarns and things or are you putting me on? Is there a big cave down under the mountain with a gold-hoard in it? Are you genuine?"

"I am not putting you on, and I am, as you so quaintly put it, gen-u-weyne, pure unadulterated dragon." My eyes turn black.

"Oh, now I've offended you, please make your eyes blue, dragon, I mean, dragon sir, I, oh wow . . ." And then there is a tear. I have smoked a bit, but now I turn my eyes blue, and she smiles.

"You *are* a prince."

"I am *not* a prince."

"If I kiss you, you won't change into anything at all?"

"I shall become a more lustful dragon." I try to affect a joking tone.

She laughs. "Where? I mean, I couldn't very well kiss you on your huge mouth, could I? I mean, how do you dragons . . . ?"

Well, that is how it went. Better to have stopped here, found some excuse to have gone back to work. But I didn't. I was too taken with my own impressiveness, and she really was very pretty, what with a nice California winter tan, her brown dark eyes, and her long straight hair. I extended my tail and cautiously curled it far around the rock, then drew it closer, so that it encompassed her. Like snakes, we are not at all slimy but rather more leathery, except somewhat softer than leather, I am told, or was about to be told, for she so remarked as she settled back against the thickness of the base of my tail.

"And quite comfortable, too," she added. The end of my tail, with its glittering triangle-spikes, now curled itself before her, and I twitched it slowly like a cat. She watched it admiringly, then ran her hand up over her head to touch one of my jeweled crests with her fingertips. "Warm ruby," she murmured. Her touch was soft. "Hey, those are really part of you. Do you . . . ?"

"Yes, of course, we grow them," I said casually.

"That's freaky," she said, and added, "but it's nice, I guess, or once I get used to the idea. Better than moles and warts, for sure!"

I agreed. (There is no truth to the rumor that our coats are such that we cannot feel. We are capable of regulating our sensitivity, even that of our rubies and amethysts.) She turned and put her cheek to my pelt. My thermostat functioned perfectly, I might add. I raised the slim tip of my tail to the vertical. Wavering sinuously like a cobra dancing to a pipe, it dipped its point to her hand, then ran up her bare forearm. The soft fuzz of hair on her arm stiffened slightly. I proceeded to maneuver my tail further up her arm to her shoulder and laid the tip upon her bare neck beneath her ear. She shivered, laid her head back upon me and said, "Ah, dragon, ah, sweet dragon."

I took the cue and answered, from Yeats,

> "If strange men come from the house
> To lead her away, do not say
> That she is happy being crazy
> Lead them gently astray."

And she whispered:

> "Escaped from bitter youth,
> Escaped out of her crowd,
> Or out of her black cloud."

And she reclined there for a few moments, her eyes closed. "You know," she said, "he wrote a poem about the dragons being no more and the hope to live that disappeared with them."

"No, that isn't quite what he said. He said that the poets kept awakening the hope to live that would have died when the dragons died off, but he was wrong about the dragons dying off, as you can see. Wrong, as man has been about us for a long time, wrong about our evil, our vulnerability to heroic swordsmen, our lust to carry off women. . . ."

"Oh?" said she, staring impertinently at my tail, which lay upon the full length of her arm.

"Well, I meant, we don't go carrying them off against their wills." I neglected to mention my *Geis*.

"You don't rape them?" She observed me, wide-eyed and smiling.

"Why, of course not." I removed my tail. I was offended. Her smile was mischievous.

"Don't be so touchy. I was only joking. So the women of all those stories *really* just came upon you in the woods, just couldn't resist you. You dragons *are* narcissistic, aren't you?"

I remained silent and she went on. "Okay, I'll stop. I guess it's true. Here I am." I still didn't say anything, but put my head down doglike on my foreclaws and stared out toward the trees. I allowed my tail, however, to loop itself about her wrist. Her wrist was small, her skin smooth. I could feel the pulse beating. Very much alive, she was.

"So we are all wrong about these things in our stories, even about dragons guarding treasures. I mean, you're just here sitting around in the country this way with nothing to do, nothing to hunt [we're vegetarians actually]. And man was really wrong about your being great guardians of the gold."

I looked at her, my eyes darkening. "Man was not that wrong," I said, quietly and firmly. I could not let her get away with that. At once, of course, I knew I had fallen for an old trick.

"I thought so," she said, and she laid her head back against me, again closed her eyes. She was very matter-of-fact about it, not at all excited. Her arm felt for my tail. She put its tip to her cheek, held it there, then brushed her lips across it. "Because you speak and you are jeweled and you breathe fire, and there has to be something somewhere, there has to be something somewhere."

We lay there a long time, while Sun descended. She fell asleep, and I felt as if I were holding her like a child. I faced the thought of what this meant. It was only techni-

cally true that I had not betrayed my *Geis*. I must see to
the work by tomorrow, for it has been said:

> Wary the wyrdhoarder:
> All wyves will wrest
> From innocent fable
> Gossip, much grief.

By the time she left it was late and had become damp
and chilly even out of the shade. She had slept, and occasionally shivered, and I had wrapped myself snugly about
her to keep her warm. When she woke, she was somewhat
startled to find me all about her, as we used to say in Ireland, but I uncoiled deftly and easily, and, if I may say so,
with something of a flourish. She was certainly impressed,
and her fear that I would express madly pythonistic ten-
dencies and squeeze her uncomfortably had vanished. I
must say that the fear never was very strong in her, and
this intrigued me.

She went away more reluctantly this time, with personal questions like where did I spend the night.

"We are nocturnal grazers," I replied to that one,
which is true enough. I was not about to say more. She
watched me closely and with great interest. She was suspicious, of course, but never pressed me beyond my cursory
answers. Something was happening all the time inside her,
though. For instance, this was the first time that she
thought to ask whether she could come back, and when.

I badly needed two days for the chests, but I didn't
want to give anything away. It would seem absurd to suggest far up here in the hills that I was all tied up without
inventing some outlandish tale about what dragons must
do or what comes upon us at full moon. I could not dis-

miss her abruptly without risk, nor did I want to. So I tried to be casual. "Come anytime," I said, and she, thank Annwn, replied that it would be a couple of days before she could probably get back. Because she had a big thing to dig some rock group in Ventura the next night. Up the hill she went, but walking slowly, thoughtfully, and turning once to look back almost sorrowfully. I began to understand that I really had this human being on my claws, as we put it.

Soon I heard her Volkswagen start. I realized that the engine as it turned over sounded the note, "blerwm, blerwm."

March 22

I think, as I work, of the White Nicors. Bombarded by the confusions of human myth, I wonder sometimes whether they ever existed, and then I regain my perspective and know that *our* myth, unlike the false human stories that insist on the existence of huge albino whales, is history and literal truth. These moments of rambling doubt, the other side of human fantasizing, are very troubling. It is a bad habit to fall into, and I must guard against it. It is my knowledge of those many human stories which corrupt Nicor history that casts an aura of doubt upon the original. And yet, for want of *Wyrd* the White Nicors did descend. Arrogant they were and, goaded by Ercllyr, constantly attacking their blue brethren, who did not have the habit of revolt or false dignity or capacity for hatred. Far in the deep the White Nicors must be, rejecting Earth and Air. They are our eternal No, the Blues our undiscriminating Yea. They wait for our failure in the dark of the sea.

Early, March 23

I know that I must work quickly, for even if she should remain discreet (and perhaps she has already spoken to someone), it is clear that there will soon be many more people wandering in these hills. Therefore, last night and the night before I hastened my efforts and began the slow movement of the first of the seven chests through the tunnels. It is a difficult job. The darkness is not the problem, for we provide our own illumination. It is the wheeling of the chests across the awkward roughness of tunnel floors. I have endlessly dragged those floors, my tail a huge scraper, and have trod them over and over to harden the base. Then I have beaten them, beaverlike, so that the wheels of the carts will not mire themselves in soft ground. Two of the chests are actually cages, and I have been most careful (as I have for centuries) with the creatures they contain. I have taken the liberty of and find satisfaction in calling these nameless creatures the Quirks and Leers respectively. I cannot go near them without profound distaste; the stunted human form of the Leers makes them grotesque. Their false, stoic calm and constant, indulgent smiles, their endless posing of abstract questions in their insipidly reasonable voices have inevitably inflicted upon me a rolling of the stomach, followed by that impulse most dangerous in a dragon, the urge to belch. I have carefully kept the Leers separated in a different alcove from the Quirks and their dark, threatening sulkiness, for I have feared that the Leers would drive the Quirks to greater and greater acts of violence, even to inflicting unspeakable torments upon each other within their own cage, perhaps upon themselves in their wrath at benevolent Leerism. Thus far I have not dared to move, and to leave unguarded in the new barrow, two chests—the first harboring the great urn of balm, one application of which will render the recipient possessed of complete bodily beauty, and the second containing the whips of spiritual perfection, capable of delivering a castigation that renders the spirit free from bodily constraint. Of the awful dangers of these two prime elements of the Hoard not enough can be said. For man to possess them is clearly for him to pervert them. They are only ideals, their achievable reality is marble coldness on the one hand and perverse tormenting masochism on the other.

Of the others, little is necessary to say here: the chests of endless life, oblivion, and boredom. Huge dangers, of course—the potentiality of the real, more than man could bear. To ask who made these chests, these identical Hoards which come into being in every district where man begins to indulge his own compelling desires, is to ask who created the desires or who created us as guarding creatures. And the only answer, no doubt, is "*Blerwm.*" Does our own virtue generate its special form of madness? To be the protectors had we to be created collectors as well? It is like the price man pays for his desire.

At the very last, I shall carry to its stunning new abode the Greater Chalice, the cup of all knowledge, closing the byways as I proceed—the byways I have so carefully and over so long a time constructed and aesthetically perfected.

Later, March 23

It is evening, and I am resting from a hard day's work during which I finally transported the Quirks and Leers. The Quirks were not as physically troublesome as I had feared. I have long suspected them to be cowards, their insults hurled at me from the protection of their cages. They sulked as usual, rolled their eyes in disgust at every enterprise I undertook, at every awkward turn, at every stumbling of the cart. They are without patience and full of hatred for the least show of incompetence or even the reasonable contemplation of any problem. Their obscene gestures and facial contortions no longer amuse me, if they ever did. I find them uninteresting. They hate me even more for this.

The Leers were worse travelers, for their dissembling is artful. I have seldom been able to endure passing any length of time in the alcove where I have kept their cage. Their tiresome and repeated debates over the most trivial and routine aspects of my treatment of them, their thoughtlessly vulgar speculations about my own bodily functions, my sex, the heat of my breath, the exact length of my tail, the allegorical suggestivity of my eyes—all carried on with such sweet and indulgent behavior toward each other and toward me—drive me quickly from them in my own display of Quirky rage. During the trip, with me pulling and occasionally pushing the cart, and scurrying about dislodging it when it became stuck, it was barely possible for me to tolerate the Leers' endless analyses of my every action, the creeping, veiled criticism of my tunnelmanship, the speculations and rhetorical questions about the viable alternatives that I had no doubt rejected. The Leers are the worst, I have often thought, and thought again, but then I have remembered the sullen, sulphurous demeanor of the Quirks and recognized the yin and yang of it, as my Eastern cousins would say. But it is not yin and yang; it is total negation. I am therefore tired.

But I am resting, too, from an odd experience, and a frightening one. It has taught me something that I must test soon under other conditions. If my suspicions are correct, my stealthy behavior these centuries has been somewhat excessive.

Near the old barrow entrance I was resting after the business with the Leers, soothing my ears, listening to the much more pleasant sound of the afternoon breeze in the trees. Waiting, too, for Lilith (her name), who had agreed to park farther away and signal her approach with a lark call, which she did rather well. She had not been sure that she could come. It would depend. I thought it might depend on whether she believed she was to be followed. I sensed that she suspected Bobby Motorcycle of curiosity and perhaps a smoldering jealousy. I was dozing, or clearing the mind, as we call it (since we do not dream), when I heard distant voices, a droning conversation. For a wild moment I thought that somehow, in some totally unexpected way, the Leers had escaped from their confinement and were strolling back through the tunnels intent, in their devastating good nature, on some inanely pedantic conversation. But just as quickly I knew the sounds to be coming from the west, where the dirt road wound down through the hills. No, these were the voices of men, human beings were coming. Then I feared that they had come for Lilith, or for whatever Lilith had told them or been made to tell them. I peered through the large aperture and protective shrubbery of my barrow entrance. There were three of them in identical Dacron blue business suits walking vaguely in my direction. I could catch a few words now at about fifty feet: water table, subdivision, split-level, black-top, easement, Hillside World.

It was a terrible moment for me. Man had come, and I had not finished my task. I had not worked steadily and rapidly enough. It would be necessary to confront these persons, drive them away, even, perhaps, to destroy them, should they persist. I acted impetuously. I left the barrow and under as much cover as possible circled quietly around so as to approach them from the rear.

I was not noticed. They rattled on about their trade, about reshaping the hills, and as the vicious talk continued, I became less indulgent of them. I thought of my friends the Oaks, and their fate, and always, of course, of Earth. I would merely frighten them as I had Bobby, if I could. Another few days was all I needed. Perhaps after their terror they would remain silent, think they had been tricked or had experienced a hallucination. I selected as a beginning a vicious snarl. In unison and suddenly the three turned about. Blank their faces for a moment. Then upon each came a huge and blatant smile, and all three stepped toward me as if I, this awesome dragon, were the most common thing in their collective experience, or as if everything out there beyond them were identical and nameless. And each began to speak, and each spoke identical words, and lo, there came over them an incredible geniality.

"Why, hello, sir, how is it we didn't notice you before?

Kinda snuck up on us, didn't ya, haha? Beautiful, isn't it, here? Just beautiful, no smog, real country living, great view prospects, no problem about water, and fine, gracious-sized lots, yes, indeed, you're lucky to come up here so early ahead of the others, you know. No problem working something out, no problem at all, haha."

I was taken aback. My mouth must have been open, my fangs showing, but it seemed not to bother them. Each was thrusting a calling card at me, approaching me with the stride of definite and devout purpose, and never a loss of the smile, or failure of nerve. I can understand it now, even observe it ironically and with some humor, but it is not the sort of thing a full-grown and stately dragon is likely to accept without surprise.

And there was no stopping them: "Here's my card, sir. I'm with Bertram, Norman, and Lopp. Welcome to Hillside World, call me Bill, John, Tom." The last in unison, of course. It came as a surprise to me that they had different names. I snorted individual balls of smoke through each nostril

"Yes, indeed," said Bill, "that's a point all right, yes, you have a point there, but look at the possibilities for resale. No problem. The price will go sky high in three years, I guarantee it."

"Guarantee it, guarantee it," said John-Tom. "And you have the choice of lots now. The view lots will go first, of course."

I blew a moderately terrifying fireball straight up in the air. Smiles all around. Laughter.

"No worries about that, no, heavens, no, they won't be moving in around here. Naturally our firm doesn't discriminate. Black, brown, polka dot. It's all the same to us. Of course," with a wink, "we don't see any of them in the business. No problem there, no, sir."

"What about dragons?" I asked.

"Dragons? Aha, well, ahem, yes haha, we might draw the line there. Depends on whether they're Asian or not, I'd say. No problem with Western dragons, haha hohoho."

And we had a good laugh all around, except that I didn't laugh, and this seemed to make them laugh even louder, to fill up the emptiness, I guess. Well, it was their job—filling up the emptiness.

They went on: "By the way, that's where the school will be. Your children of school age? The district's already contracted for the land. Good walk for the kids. Say, isn't this air bracing? Out of the smog, no dust bowl. It's really the place. Now, on this terrain you could build a real interesting home, with the pool down there. What was your name, sir? Didn't catch the name, haha."

My astonishment was complete, so complete that I answered, suppressing a flame, "Firedrake." John-Tom made a note, Bill answered: "Drake—well, Fred, I'd sure get in on this thing right away. It's the best deal in Southern California land right now, a real good deal. It's just *real* fine. Now where can I reach you when we go on the market with the view lots? Phone? I'll call you first on the list." So I improvised a phone number in Santa Barbara, we shook claws all around, I was slapped on my major amethyst, and they wandered off up the hill in a vaguely eastern direction chatting amiably with each other, now that they weren't laughing, pointing at trees and rocks, hillsides, and valleys. And I heard one in the distance shout, "Say, there's a big pond over there; why, we could dam up this area over here and have a real nice natural lake, with some filling and digging. Say, I don't think old Ed knows this is here."

Just then Lilith came from the road, running this time, and the men had turned and were walking back toward the barrow entrance. I froze like a lizard for a second, hoping they would veer off before I had to take action. Lilith had stopped too, watching them and watching me. Then she ran toward them. They turned, stopped. She spoke quietly to them. I could not hear what they were saying. She was pointing toward the road and making gestures of helplessness. Then all four of them walked up the hill toward her car. She was talking rapidly, and they were laughing and generally quipping, I suppose. I heard nothing more until two cars started up. First Lilith's Volks, and shortly thereafter some larger type. Both drove off.

I loped to the barrow in relief. I knew that Lilith had grasped the situation and somehow turned them away from the barrow at the last moment before I would have had to do something drastic. But it also meant that she knew where the barrow was.

Early Morning, March 24

There is an old dragon story that Ceugant met Modred long ago in Wales and cast a spell upon him so that Modred could not see him. In short, it says that we are sometimes invisible; I think I have now grasped the story's symbolism. In this case it is actually man who casts the spell. I also now understand how human myths of men turning into dragons, and vice versa, may have developed. It is simply a matter of how men see. But I am speaking into this thing not to be philosophical but to record that Lilith came back an hour or so after the real-estate salesmen had gone. I met her at the barrow entrance, for she had come directly there.

"Thank you for sending them off," I said.

"Oh, yeah, well, I gave them the car-trouble bit. I didn't want you having to eat them up or whatever you do. Broil them, perhaps." She smiled shyly.

"We're vegetarians, except for fish, and that's only when we're aquatic," I offered.

"I guess you don't want me to come into your cave; at least you're standing there in the way, sorta."

I was, though my eyes were definitely blue and not the purple of Hoard-guarding. The problem is that you can't stand casually if you are a four-legged creature, and she didn't appreciate the more subtle dragon nuances. Nor could she ever learn all of them, such as those having to do with our electronic system.

"I shouldn't let you in, but if you promise to touch nothing, you can come as far as the Outer Hall."

She laughed at that. Thought I was joking. But when we went down from the small, crudely hollowed antechamber I could tell she was impressed. And why not? Well, first of all, the tunnel alone is a modestly psychedelic experience. I've used army-surplus white as a base. It is easy enough to come by in large lots. The designs themselves I have worked at freely over the years. We dragons were doing the abstract thing a century before man, inspired by our dragonesses and the intricate designs of our own hides. In the Outer Hall itself is much of my wrought-iron work,

of which two large hanging lamps are perhaps the best examples. The Hall also contains in a corner my forge and
anvil.

"Groovy," she said, looking about. (I must come to accept this term of respect as one of the facts of modern life.)
She wandered around the hall for a bit, then flopped on a
corner couch. I haunched, facing her, and thought about
producing a smile, thought better of it. Though the venti-
lating system of the halls is adequate for dragons, I was
not sure of what the human response might be to the
smoke. She was grinning.

"This is some digs. I had no idea you'd done all this
back in here. Why, I'd expected, you know, a well, like a
barrow, or something, just a hole. But—say, you're
pretty talented. You make all these things?"

"In my spare time, yes," I said, examining a foreclaw.

"Well, what else do you have? I mean, you just graze
and then sleep, don't you, like, what else is there for dragons?" Pause. Eyes sharpened: "Say, how long have you
been here?"

I didn't really want to entertain these questions, and
besides, I now realized that Lilith was a lot more percep-
tive than I had taken her to be. In fact, she was a pretty
cagey type. And all that groovy, like, I mean, and you
know talk wasn't going to fool me one bit in the future.
She went on, saying she didn't understand why I had
taken all the trouble when I didn't really need the space.
As she said it I noticed her observing the passageways off
from the hall, and she was saying slyly maybe I did need
the space, did I have a family, like was I married, or did
dragons do that, and were there children, and what was I
doing all alone 'way out here in California in a big place I

had hollowed out of the hills? She was eyeing me in a new way; suddenly she seemed aggressively dangerous.

Precisely as the *Blerwm* has warned: any human being would eventually press his luck, sensing that I held something he did not have. Nevertheless, with Lilith—in the face of the particular instance—I was surprised.

I could tell that she sensed my attitude of distrust, so she ceased her questioning. She stared at me solemnly. "You don't want to answer all those questions," she said.

I was afraid she would sulk. Something told me that she could be very unpleasant in a sulk. So I answered, "Not all of them, at least not yet. But I'll start with the family and all that." And I did. I had thought frequently about large bodies of fresh water recently, specifically about Lough Corrib, and I described it, and my trip to Lough Mask, without explaining the dragon trials. All the time a strong current of precise memory flowed through me, particularly as I thought of Gwynfyd.

A profoundly impressive dragoness she was, of color deep blue, streaked with gold, her tongue of chartreuse, her hide of sinuous smoothness, her capacities for blue flame immense, her eyes of deep and varying color as she talked, quietly, softly. Of dragon lore she was the mistress, of the great pythonosophy she had total intellectual control. The conversation of our eyes was of the whole spectrum, and when we loved beneath Mask's waters the surface was brought to a turmoil and even the larger fish finned to the most obscure recesses of the lake. Human beings on the shore spoke with wonder then of deep monsters in the Lough. To make love to a dragoness is beyond human understanding. They are strong, dragonesses, nearly as strong as we, and in combat more vicious by nature. Their capacity for outrage far exceeds ours. Sinuous they are, with great strength of squeezing and movements quick as lightning. Smaller of body, proportionately longer and slimmer of tail than we, they employ the cauda with great dexterity, as a whip, a lever, an arm, a sexual object. Wound around my trunk, Gwynfyd's tail, in the moment of passion, in its shuddering and grasping, would require a flexing struggle simply for me to breathe. I still possess at the base of my neck the scar of one of her fangs from our first encounter. It was on Corrib's shore that I first came upon her alone. We had known, of course, of our betrothal, and now, the proper time passed, we were prepared to meet. She sunned herself at full length near the water, waiting. The gold tints of her slim body glittered. She dozed, but she was immediately aware of my presence. When I approached within breathing distance she growled deeply, but did not move. I circled her slowly and ever closer, while she growled continuously. Then suddenly her tail lashed out and caught mine with a great slap and whipping coil. With all my strength I rushed to pull her into the lake while she clawed the ground seeking a hold on the shore. But I prevailed, and as we entered the water we were thrown into an embrace of the whole body. It was then that she scarred me.

All of this I did not describe to Lilith, except to say that we dragons were mated at about age one hundred, that we practiced strict birth-control principles, that Gwynfyd had produced one son, which was our proper allotment according to dragon *Wyrd*, that my dragoness remained in Ireland going about her various tasks, including the teaching of pythonosophy to the young—a duty thought best performed by the female of our species rather than by the more sanguine male—that such separations were the common practice of dragons, that it had been said I would return to live in Corrib but exactly when was uncertain—the actual sign not having been given.

I had thought that sufficient. Indeed, it was too much, for I had certainly implied that it was not in dragon character to come all the way to California on a lark, that there was some definite purpose in my voyage. But Lilith had become quiet and did not venture to quiz me on my actions. We were silent for a while.

Then I learned that I could count on one thing consistently triumphing over her curiosity about me; that was her preoccupation with human problems. These creatures were fundamentally egocentric.

"You dragons had to solve your population problem, and you did. You just went ahead and did." She said it not so much to me as to the world. I could not tell whether it made her feel better, made her consider that man might solve his problem, too, or threw her into greater despair over the disorganization of human effort.

"Of course, it wasn't quite the problem for us that it is for you. I mean, if you have ever, well, ever had intercourse with a dragoness, it's not, it's not the sort of thing you can get up for, if you'll pardon the expression, every day, or every month. One sleeps for some time afterwards, and that's the reason, partly, that we leave our mates when we come to——"

She watched me, and smiled broadly with a covetous satisfaction and said, "Guard your treasures, because you can't be caught napping, you've got to be vigilant. Please, dragon, please, let me see your treasure. It's down one of those hallways, isn't it?"

She saw I was frowning, which is to say that my eyes were purpling, so she added, "Of course, I'd be scared to go *alone,* I'd never go alone. Besides, I'd never be able to figure out which hall to take, and——" I relaxed a bit, my tail coiled again after stiffening. The old dragon *Wyrd* had been renewed in me, though, and she knew it.

"Okay, okay, I just thought I'd ask. I won't say anything more about it, I swear. It's a secret between you and me." The ominous verses of Knäckerune on human secrets thundered in my mind, but I accepted her words with composed silence. Our conversation ceased for some minutes. I feared that she was falling into despondency.

"It's going to be, like it'll be Armageddon," she said. "I mean it just can't continue on this way. Like look what's happening or isn't happening. Nothing ever gets *done.* People are being born, and no one dies any more to speak of, and the air's terrible, and all the fish in Lake Erie are dead. I remember Grandpa talking about Lake Erie white-fish, and now they just *don't exist,* hardly. Animals are dying out, and you just can't *invent* them! Pretty soon *we* won't exist. We're going to squeeze ourselves and suffocate ourselves to death. It makes you wanta tear out and do something, but there's nothing to do, is there? So——"

"So, here you are up in the hills talking to a dragon."

It was a weak answer, and I was ashamed of it. Somehow, with the control *we* have over our own lives one might expect us to do better by human beings in the way of practical advice or even philosophical reflection, particularly since this was one of my excuses for continuing to see her. As it seemed to be turning out, we could keep some of the primal horrors from them, but they were creating new ones of their own. They might even make Earth

82

uninhabitable for us, though our toleration of smog exceeded theirs.

Therefore, her answer was sarcastic: "Yeah, isn't that quaint? You guys should have died out long ago."

"Yes, of course, we are quaint creatures. And it may appear to you we should have died out like the dinosaur. He was squeezed out, I believe, but we solved our problems, and we *are* rather adaptable. It's a long story why we're here. Have you ever thought that perhaps everything, even man, was supposed to die out long ago, that the odds were against everything, and they're still against everything? Anyway, we didn't go, even after my species came up from the sea and changed its ways drastically."

It *was* a long story, and I found myself telling it. A human being was hearing it perhaps for the first time: I began with the First Ceugant and the Great Council of millenniums ago, all the proceedings of which every young dragon is obliged to memorize and recount as the Second Trial. The First Ceugant presided, and there were dragons from the whole of the world assembled in every lake and tarn of Western Europe. Spread over that map, we were all tuned in on the general wave length. Thus we avoided making it one of those mad humanoid get-togethers in which hundreds of thousands of people clog the highways and sit in the rain and sun in fields just to commune together. Of course they aren't electrified, and they're basically more anarchic than we. (I reminded myself that I ought to tune in Feuerkugel. Hadn't talked with him in days.) It was not as if we had no idea of what had to be done. First, there was the dragon population, which threatened to get out of control. Then, if this tendency were not checked there would be the problem of breath control. The council was called at this time primarily because there were reports of quarrels among dragons over the great Hoards of the East and West. That, too, was brought about by a surfeit of dragons.

It was not greed, as some may think and man has written, that caused these quarrels, but the problem of providing for each dragon his proper occupation beyond grazing and sex. If enough guarding were not provided, or if the pythonosophy were not predicated upon the assumption that to guard was our nature, then the spectacle of the obese dragon would become common, the population would further rise, and there really would be dragons ravaging the countryside. Every dragon knew this. Every one of us recognized that whatever we decided must acknowledge the guarding instinct. We admitted it and were ready to go on from there. Further, we knew that universal collectioneering had to be acknowledged as policy, for scavenging too easily exploded into ravaging when it was pent up. In the early days, of course, collectioneering was put to direct social use. Dragons kept Earth free of human refuse. But there are too many people discarding now for us to be effective. Our collecting cannot keep up. It can only express itself today as compulsion or connoisseurship. Being aesthetes we choose the latter and thus discipline our natural tendency. We transform trash to art when we can and complete its becoming where men have misunderstood the aim of production. Perhaps this is mere self-justification for curious behavior, but I believe not. We still aim to make Earth ready for Draco's last dining.

Lilith was thoughtful as she listened. She said, "Our problem is, well, we just don't have any idea of ourselves, I mean as a species. And all the theories leave something out. We don't know what we are or even where we are, I guess."

"That brought about the great dragon epic."

"Hey, that's cool, you mean you have creative writers and all that?"

I explained that we didn't write it out, that we all knew it in our powerful memories. I explained the *Great Blerwm* and how it was commissioned by the Council and was originally conceived of as a blue-ribbon panel report, but the Great Knäckerune reported back that every time his group addressed itself to a particular phase of the dragon problem (a term later expunged from the record), his own attempt at purely analytical language so offended him that he ended up composing a piece of verse satirizing his own procedures. So our natural tendency to be poetry-making creatures prevailed at the outset. And the Council learned more of itself from this. We made the first anti-definition of ourselves.

"What's that? A definition of what you aren't?"

"Oh, no, it's a rejection of definition itself as a mode of self-knowledge. We had a very short time of it with pure analytics as an effective social device. But, of course, we're dragons, not men, and there are some things that we just simply came to know. It's our nature."

"I wonder if it could be true of us and what those things are," she mused.

"No doubt there's some limited applicability," I said, seeking a detached attitude in my language, and regretting it. It is improper to offer the dissimulation of a reply to such a question. The dragon knows too much of man, because he knows what rests in the great treasures. Some men have come near self-knowledge. Some have nearly conjured in their minds a dragon's Hoard complete with urns and chalices—after performing the enormous human feat of eliminating from their minds the conventional pictures of piled coins and jewels. And they have put these visions into a few poems of occasionally accomplished verse. Only they have come near to the truth. But their audiences have been few, and their reputations of little account among the civil great. The idea of a treasure that must *not* be opened, must be held at a distance by the imagination, is current only among a few, if any.

"Dragons are rational beasts, really," she said.

"No, we have simply come upon anti-definition and what we call a prophecy of ourselves as song. We have decided, because after establishing the song nothing else was thinkable, or actable, to be what the song insists. It's very hard to explain in the language. I'm sorry, I know it doesn't make sense. It sounds too much like what man calls superstition." The only thing to do was to sing it, but it would have taken far too long, and there would be endless misunderstandings.

"I was thinking all that, sorta, because nothing you've said yet is superstitious. You're a, well, a rational beast. Oh, I'm sorry, that word again. I can't get rid of it, maybe." My eyes had turned purple, because of the Leers.

"No, my dear, that distinction between reason and emotion is all wrong. We don't recognize it for dragons. Our song rejects it. Who's ever heard of a good, I mean a *really* good song that's all feeling and no reason or all reason and no feeling? Assuming, of course, the words can be made to refer to anything in the first place. It's impossible. Through our songs we know that." That's why pythonosophy is verse and song and thought all rolled into one, but I didn't go into the technicalities.

"Why don't we know that?"

"You're assuming it's the same for dragons and men. If it were, we could say you have not prophesied adequately in song. But I suspect it isn't the same."

I had made her no happier, if that was what she was looking for; and being young and human, she probably was. That was part of the problem. We were a quite different species, and though we could speak their language, we were without the interior struggles some of the recent human half-prophets had made books on. But even if they could anti-define themselves into adequate prophecy of their own torn and struggling existences, and even if they could debunk the theme of the pursuit of happiness, even then it was likely that they would come upon important and tragic differences between dragon and human nature.

I mentioned the pursuit of happiness bit. I said we didn't think much of it. It wasn't one of the things that were even metaphysically ideal, meaning, of course, I didn't have that item in the chests. Funny, it cheered her up for a moment to consider it that way, and she thought she'd captured some happiness, I guess. I reflected on the frustrations of dealing with these creatures, as prophesied by Knäckerune in the twelfth epistle, Book Ten. I reflected also that I could not go on much longer with this talk, because we dragons had our *Wyrd* and knew ourselves by it, through the acting of it, that is, and not through endless discussion of it, which was *Geis*. In the ideal world man would prophesy his own nature, his own acts, as we dragons have managed to do

But I did answer one question:

"You mean you dragons all came to agreement at the Great Council, and you've kept it? That's extraordinary."

I sighed. She had not quite understood that dragon

agreements simply are not broken. "Yes, what else was there for us to do but to know ourselves? It is our nature." Perhaps she would never quite understand. I thought pityingly of this.

It is the wrong frame of mind for a dragon.

Later, March 24

I shall say a little more of what transpired in the long conversation between us. She was thoughtful and perplexed and alternately amused and sad at my disclosures. Amused when she thought she recognized a wonderful fiction, like Swift's Houyhnhnms or some human utopia; perplexed, I think, when it came back to her that she was actually sitting there *talking with a dragon,* who was real and who probably wasn't simply telling her crazy stories, if she wasn't freaked out herself. When she decided to leave, after midnight, it seemed to me that she had grown up, whether for the good I could not tell.

Still later, March 24

My speech to the recorder was interrupted by distant noises and I had to investigate them. It was just as well; I should have been at work on the chests early instead of attending to my memoirs. The noises were people again, and they were very near the barrow. I was quickly at the entrance, tail stiffened, eyes deep purple. Two men again, in blue Dacron suits again, stood about twenty yards away with their backs to me, looking out over the little valley which was, I presumed, to become part and parcel of Hillside World. I could catch some of their conversation. One of them was saying:

"We tried that in Delaware, but the exhaust mechanism just wouldn't do the job, and then Otis flew up from Houston, told us to scrap the whole damned mess and start over, and we'd just started when Chicago called and broke up the whole team, so we never got very far on it. And that's why I'm here now. . . ."

I ventured forth and, as yesterday, snarled and smoked. The two turned around and stared. They were taken aback, but they were not frightened. For a strange moment again I couldn't believe it. They came forward with quizzical expressions on their faces, as if presented with some curious out-of-the-way puzzle.

"What kind of a contraption is that, Herb?"

"Looks like one of those old steamers. Someone's been up here and set a fire in it, I guess. Sorta crude. I suppose it's left over from some earlier settlers. Funny, though, there's no old houses around here or anything else like that. It's pretty deserted."

"Yeah, you see these crazy machines out in the hills where people have tried to homestead or there's been a mining outfit or something."

"Boy, I can't think of who'd make this! It's for the Smithsonian. You know, we ought to get the maintenance boys from the lab to come up here and pick it up."

"What for, an antique?"

"No, put it in one of those glass cases like they do with old fire engines or something—out in front of the lab."

This time I didn't have to experience the whole range of astonishment that had come over me with the real-estate people. So I froze rigid and prepared to allow whatever casual inspection was to follow. I assumed they'd go away after a time, and they did. They strolled off casually, discussing what lot they'd put in for if and when this place really began to move. The last word with reference to me was that, you know, this old relic isn't in bad shape. At least they were puzzled over what my function was, but that didn't seem to bother them very much. This was California, I was allocated to the past, and they were on their lunch hour.

Products of the age of cybernetics, prophets of plastic and transistors, these creatures. Men of intense training, stunningly professional they were, with the curiosity of their kind for whatever work there is to be done, as one ad intones. As they walked back up to the road I hurried to the barrow. There were two chests to be moved today, and perhaps Lilith would return at evening. I worried no more about the two visitors, I did not even see them out of sight. They would not discover the entrance.

Early, March 25

I am working much faster now, far in the depths of the hills, moving the chests of Endless Life, Boredom, and Oblivion through the dark passages. I am working rapidly because of Lilith and my fear that she will come to know ever and ever more about my activities now that she comes and goes confidently in the Outer Hall of my domain.

My domain: a curious concept, that, engendered by my having lived solitary yet within reach of all human media, which are saturated with it. A territorial animal the human being apparently is, staking out curious abstract claims on the shifting land. Feuerkugel, too, has noticed how this abstract territorialism has come to invade his own feelings, how it threatens to corrupt the purity of our relationship to the treasures we so carefully guard. For as dragons we consider that we own nothing, but keep all we guard in trust for man and thus for Earth itself. The *Blerwm* teaches that Earth is a point, that the triangle's apex alone is real, that the base is merely its imaginative expansion. Each of us on Earth's surface lives on a piece of that expansion, emanation of the central Earth core. At that core all space is really one, every parcel of land is collapsed back into the great microcosmic center from where it came. We hold the emanation in trust. We do not own Earth, each of us merely expresses constantly some different aspect of this fundamental unity.

Dragons, therefore, do not really understand the concept of property, of ownership. It is to us the most telling example of the limitations of human understanding that human beings cannot transcend their idea of the material solidity of Earth to grasp its living, ever-changing character. All of their attempts at surveying, at map-making, at legal declarations of ownership are quaint to us. Land and ocean change. Every human being might meditate upon the tidelands and the unruly impertinence of the sea.

Thus I have resisted considering these halls my own. They are themselves, and they proceed back, as does everything, to that central point. Farther and farther outward from that center the square of land that a man erroneously calls his own extends into airier and airier substance and becomes larger and larger until its size is infinite and defies the imagination with its sublimity. As from the smallest point all proceeds, so the most sublime hugeness is nothing. There is no ownership of these things, only imaginative grasp of this truth and the holding in trust for nature of that which one has cultivated or reworked. Thus I resist, and Feuerkugel resists, the desire to preserve what we know will always change and shift, for land and sea are alive and will move.

I have never marked out, even in my mind, the spatial limits of a domain here. True, I collect the strange excreta of human civilization. It is *our* imperfection, or our anachronism. I may only discipline it. Perhaps there is some fabulous beast unknown to us guarding the chalice, which, were I to locate it and drink therefrom, would relieve me of our strange drive. But what then would I be? Is not my madness to transform trash an inevitable accompaniment of my strength? What guardianship could I perform without it? What could Earth have entrusted to me? Who would, in turn, protect man's spirit from the perfection of oblivion?

Later, March 25

Oblivion is the lightest of the chests, so I have chosen to take it last of the three. Today I have moved rock-heavy Boredom a good distance through the tunnels. I had been very busy, almost in a fury of possession, for several hours when Lilith returned. She found me distant. It took a while for me to get into the mood for humantalk. It is really a great strain on us, speaking with those terms humanosophy has somehow built into the language with brick and mortar.

She wanted, as apparently most human beings do, to talk about herself, with a speech addressed to how she didn't know (sigh) whether she was a radical today or not. Yesterday yes, she had definitely been a radical, for all the smog blew in and there was a four-hour traffic jam on the freeway and the President and his whole cabinet flew out to San Clemente with those hundreds of newsmen and Rafferty gave a speech on football scholarships, berating long-haired madmen who were, of course, the only ones against them. And everybody clapped and shouted and resolved to fire all the Red professors everywhere. And the identical things had happened a year ago. So yesterday she was very, very radical, and bugged Bobby unmercifully, calling him an anachronism on a steel horse, for no good reason except he wouldn't play her involvement game. Then Bobby had told her yesterday the hell with it all, it was all a pile of shit and he wanted her to get on the motorcycle with him and simply get the hell out of there.

"Where is 'out of there'?" I asked.

"That's why I didn't go. I didn't know where it was either, but there are lots of people going there. I wanted to go, and I guess it's why I like Bobby—because he wants to go—but when I'm this radical nut it isn't right and I bug him. Say, you know there's just messes of people wandering around these hills now. This used to be 'out of there,' but now it's getting to be 'there,' or something. Like down a few miles. I saw lots of people just walking around in the fields."

"Yes, I know. I've felt that."

"Hey, like you just sense they're there somehow? That's cool how you do that. But hadn't you better think about moving?"

"I am moving," I said.

"Gee, that's too bad, it must make you angry-sad to see your place, or lair, or whatever you call it, abandoned. I mean, just left. It doesn't seem fair."

"Unfair to dragons," I quipped.

"Yeah, why not protest? Give 'em a fireball. Run 'em off your land."

"No, it isn't that way at all with us. We don't own this land. We have no concept of owning the land."

"But, then, it's not theirs either."

"No, it's not theirs."

"Gee, you're sort of a utopian beast, aren't you? I mean I guess talking to you is like talking with a book sometimes. You've got a sort of communism, you dragons."

I've never liked the word "beast" very much, but I did not dwell upon it. The term "communism" did get to me, though. It only muddied the clarity of the whole dragon respect for Earth. The communistic and capitalistic ideas were equally human and equally frail. "No," I answered, "dragonism isn't communal ownership of anything. It's ownership of the land by Earth. It's acknowledgment of this otherness as having a prior right, no, even more than that, having the only right. The sanction isn't in history, it's in being."

"Then man isn't the measure of all things."

"My dear, even dragons do not measure all things. Nothing measures all things."

"But you guard things," she said shyly. Had she been

watching me at work? "Like *treasures*," she said, and her eyes were large and shining, and, it seemed to me that they just barely failed to turn gray, which is our collecting color.

"Quite humanoid," I snorted. "Greedy for treasure. Do you want it in gold, silver, or paper green?"

"Oh, no, oh no, it isn't that, not that at all!" and she looked down at her hands folded on her lap. "I didn't mean that. I don't think you understand. It's just the idea of your being here and guarding a treasure, not something to find and despoil or use or be a miser with. It's just the wonderful idea of you being here like—like——"

"Like the old stories? It's the wonder of it?" I'll admit I was touched by this. Even after all the malignity with which we dragons have been treated in those stories, I found myself elated by her desire to mythicize me, puffed up a bit by it, even as I disapproved of it. It was a curious feeling. We dragons have suffered from this problem ever since man began perpetrating mythic inaccuracies about us. I am fascinated by our public image in the human imagination and yet it is annoying to realize that man has never grasped the amazing nature of our *reality*. What I am trying to say is that we dragons consider ourselves the nearest thing to a *real* fabulous creature in existence.

I proceeded to offer the most contemptible cliché, probably out of embarrassment at my own thoughts: "But look at the wonder of space exploration, and all that. Why, you live in a world where there are all sorts of wonders discovered all the time."

"That's the trouble, isn't it," she said. "Somehow when we capture it, it's not a wonder any longer, and—well, you know, our imagination loses control of it, sorta."

"That's why I shall keep my treasure from you, of course."

"Yes, of course, yeah, I guess so, but it's really confusing. It's as if we have only what we don't really have, like if you become too human then I have to go home and think you up into a fabulous dragon again. I keep turning you into a person. You know, I don't think I like the human mind! What if I'd seen you at a distance and remembered that and thought all my life, gee I really saw a dragon? So I'd have this strange secret, and maybe even tell a few people about it, but they'd only think I was crazy."

"I'm not sure. A few might be a little jealous. Back in their own imaginations there'd always be the possibility you'd really seen me, and you'd have contributed something to them in a way. You'd have kept their imaginations in trust, so to speak."

"But the more often I told it, the farther away it would be, somehow. And you'd become obscure and mechanical like cybernetics keeps telling us we are."

There was a curious circularity about the whole process that she was getting to with her talk. I admired her insight; my hope for her was rekindled. I told her about the two space engineers who'd mistaken me for a boiler, and how they'd reached beatitude already. She laughed about it, because I hammed it up with a good deal of comic indignation, and it *was* funny. But in a way I was proving her point. I was corrupting the real situation by reworking it for my audience. I was casting my present state of mind upon it. She became solemn.

"Your story makes me sad," she said.

"Not for me, I hope. I've regained my dignity, I think."

"No, not for you, for man."

I looked at her gently. I wished to wrap my tail about her again and hold her, but I knew that I had better not. I would only be humanizing myself in her eyes. And of course it was far, far too late to invoke dragon fright in her now and drive her away—not with what she knew of me. She had before her a real, speaking dragon, and we would have to make the best of it, for her sake.

Yet as I acknowledged all of this I knew that she had come far too close to the treasure, and perhaps to her own destruction.

March 26

She stayed in the Outer Hall last night, curled asleep on a pile of pillows in a corner, while I went on with my work. All night I was at it. She had promised not to go beyond the room, because our conversation was still impressed upon her mind. Maybe she has come to realize that actually to see the treasure (or whatever it is I protect deep in Earth) would be some sort of mistake. Today, after heavy work, we walked outside with the intention of going to the rock. I had considered a swim, but the tarn was probably a little too chilly for her in March, and I might well frighten her with the churning of the waters. We tend to let ourselves go in a swim. As we parted the bushes at the barrow entrance, my tail suddenly stiffened straight out and I turned my eyes purple again. At once I sent Lilith back to the Outer Hall. It seemed that you couldn't step outdoors any more without someone interrupting.

Not far away there were two strollers. One was bearded, wearing a beret and gold-rimmed glasses, and carrying a walking stick. The other was much younger, bearded, wild of hair. Both were dressed in various forms of army-surplus gear, quite familiar to me, as is all surplus. They were on some sort of hike, but it was a slow and ambling one, each walking with head down, the younger with hands clasped behind his back, each foot going forward slowly almost as if to test the ground. And they walked over the terrain not in a straight line or along some plotted course but in a wandering way.

"Yes," I heard the older one say, "ahem, yes indeed, epistemology is dead."

"Is phenomenology dead?" asked the younger.

"Phenomenology is dead," the older replied.

"God is dead," said the younger.

"Well, Kierkegaard is dead," said the older.

There was a pause, they had walked nearly in a circle, thinking.

"Santayana says——" exclaimed the younger suddenly.

"He's dead," the older chided. "A long time now."

"Marx, Engels, Lenin, Trotsky," the younger one shouted, in great agitation, his huge black hat bobbing back on his head.

"All dead," said the older.

"Wittgenstein," said the young man, composing himself.

"Only remains, snips of paper. Dead," chided the older.

"Austin, Ayer, Ryle," the young man pleaded.

"A-live?" the older sneered.

"Marcooooooooooooooooose!" the younger screamed, waving his arms and hopping about.

"Really," the older scorned.

Screaming "Mao, Mao," the young man turned upon him. The older brandished his cane, shouting, "Down, down, down."

And then the younger was sobbing, sinking to his knees, sobbing. I could detect a few phrases—"transform the society," "creative role," "the whole community," "control over our own lives"—rolling forth among the sobs. The older was poking a wildflower now with his walking stick, his back to the young man, who was prostrate, fists clenched, beating the ground, shouting, "Thou, thou, thou!"

The older man then turned in a vaguely purposeless way and stared directly at me. He shouted suddenly, "Look at that! Why, look at that!" The younger jumped up and stared in my direction. My tail stiffened again as they came toward me. Suddenly I realized that it was not I they were walking toward.

"It's a *ceanothus arboreus,* an excellent example of the species. About to bloom," the older said.

"I say," said the younger. They had seen right through me! I say they had seen right through me to a bush the older man wished to examine! They had not seen *me* at all!

Later, March 26

When I told her this story her answer was: "So dragons are dead. What else is new?" She had laughed nervously and tried to make an ironic joke of it, but in truth I believe she was a little put out by the behavior of the humanosophers, the engineers, and the real-estate agents. She was annoyed at humankind.

After a while she remarked that if she'd seen a dragon,

why hadn't they? But she countered the question herself by deducing what had only recently come clear to me: "No, they saw what they allowed themselves to see. But then, maybe you're not a dragon at all and I just make you into one. Maybe I *want* you to be a dragon and you're really a—a——"

"A what?" I pressed, because I was really interested to know. But, as any competent psychoanalyst or even reporter will tell you, I had made a mistake. I had broken into the movement of her thought, and now she was silent.

She was staring intently at me, trying to exorcise the dragon, I thought, hoping to find something else there. Was she beginning to think that all those stories about people who assumed dragon shapes, like Fafnir, were really allegories of her own experience? Or was she coming to be critical of her desire to romanticize things and wanted me instead to turn into some old desert rat of the hills, or a crazy hermit living in a cave?

As she stared, tears came to her eyes again. She put her face in her hands. "I want you to be a dragon, and I— I want you to be human, too. But I *don't* want to be like them, thinking you into those other shapes, even into objects." I thought at that moment, and I think now as I report all this, that in some ways the world would be better for her if she could kiss me and I were to turn into a wonderful prince. But she could have her wish only if the world had been made in such a way that there was no treasure to guard, only if it were possible for man to achieve all desire and still be man.

Things are as they are.

In any case, the first reaction to someone in Lilith's state is uncomplicated. It is an urge to ease the torment by soothing balms. We dragons know there is no balm of any account that is not dangerous (we guard the most dangerous of all). Nor dared I offer the chalice of complete knowledge. Yet I said to myself (and this was compounding my past errors) that a bit more knowledge might really enable her to organize her conflict into some sort of personal prophecy. I said that to myself despite my realization that our relationship had been changing. Less often do I observe her watching me as if I were some magnificent work of visionary imagination, requiring appreciation. Now she seems to be watching me as if I were a dragon guarding a treasure that might be of considerable value on the market. I, in turn, must not treat her as a visionary child. Yet the visionary child is somehow still there underneath to torment me. I hoped that in carrying her a little farther toward knowledge she could reach some new plateau. Foolish indeed! Does not the appreciation of cosmic conflict make man weep the more? Is not this what I am learning from her?

Therefore, when she asked me again to see the Great Hall, I acquiesced, and I explained at the same time that most of the treasure had been moved.

Off the Outer Hall, where Lilith spent the night, there are several passages, some leading nowhere in particular, some doubling back and intersecting others. One, and one only, leads to the Great Hall lower down in Earth, from which branch the seven alcoves. Until recently each had harbored one of the seven chests. I led Lilith down the passageway to the Great Hall. We stopped to peer into side rooms where I had stored some of those things dearest to my scavenging. Third on the left struck her most. It was there with much labor that I had installed the husks of my Marmon, Cord, and Ultimate Model T. The Cord, rescued

from an accident, I had spent much time repairing—
hammering, welding, painting. It had no engine. That I
had left in the dump, judging it beyond saving. Its sleek
body, set against that of the stately Marmon, was a brilliant sight. Even so, it has never really moved me. The
Marmon has always struck me as more admirable. The Ultimate T, if ever finished, will be sublime.

Brimming with desire to communicate, I tried to make
these distinctions meaningful to Lilith as I crouched there
while she went all about the autos, feeling them, getting
inside behind the wheel, genuinely interested in them, but
as period pieces, I am afraid. My argument about the T's
sublimity didn't seem to impress her. Perhaps it was simply that she had never seen a dragoness, whose form provides a lesson and a standard.

I was compelled to a reckless act. I decided to take her
to the alcove housing the chest of balm, for it contained
my fresco of Gwynfyd. After spending much time preparing a suitable wall and collecting the proper colors, I had
worked for years at perfecting the likeness. It had not been
my first venture, of course, in the fine arts. The Great Hall,
across which I led Lilith, is covered with a variety of what
human beings would call mythological and I call correc-
tive or historical paintings, done in various styles. I had
begun my career with a large wall painting of the dragon
vanquishing St. George. This is the St. George who human
mythology says fought and vanquished a dragon on Duns-
more Heath. In the picture I give to the saint—who had
never been to England, incidentally, so it is clear that
someone else fought this dragon—nevertheless, to St.
George I give the magic sword Ascalon, with which
human mythology erroneously credits him slaying numerous of our kind across the whole face of Europe and north-

ern Africa. But in this battle the huge and handsome dragon, heavily-tailed and ruby-scaled right to the tip, has wound his tail around the fanatic knight's wrist, rendering arm and sword useless. Knowing the end is in sight, the saint crosseth himself with his free left hand, and is uttering, in the balloon above (the only aspect of the painting that does not identify it with the style of Giotto), a traditional anti-dragon curse—"Devour thy tail, O dragon!"—which has absolutely no effect, no dragon in recorded dragonography having ever so done, either under the influence of curse or by his own desire. On the other hand, the traditional words of exorcism would have been as pointless: "Exorciso te immunde Spiritus." They are designed for demons, which we are not. Besides, dragons are notoriously, fastidiously clean, though much maligned in alchemy as the gross material from which the purity of gold is drawn. Only someone obsessed with gold could refer to our jewels as gross. On the other hand, if the gold of alchemy is taken as symbolic of what we do guard, then we know why no alchemical experiment ever succeeded. The stories are wish-fulfillment dreams. What would knowledge be worth, golden or otherwise, if there were nothing still to seek?

Well—to return to last night. I apologize for becoming so exercised over these wretched misrepresentations. When Lilith saw the painting I could tell that she was moved. She sat cross-legged on the floor of the Great Hall and stared up at the titanic combat. I watched her face. Serious it was, thoughtful, despite the domineering blankness of youth. She sat there for several minutes without moving. I paced around behind her expecting a verdict to be rendered upon my art.

"Well," she said, "he was putting up a brave fight. Think of taking on a dragon like that with only your puny sword."

I should have expected that. Through her eyes it was a matter of poor George caught in the clutches of an unmerciful fiend. Never a thought as to who started it, as to what the hell St. George was doing hunting dragons, as to why human beings, let alone saints, should decide to wage total war on dragons and to suppress them forever, even wipe them out if they had their way.

But I swallowed my annoyance and asked, "What do you think of the overall form? It has its crudities, but I believe the design of it comes off." Of course, the dragon, with his sinuous folds and curves, was the dominating organizational force in the picture, as well as its hero. I felt I could impel her to some remarks about him.

"Yeah, that's neat, all right. Like how those masses complement the ones down there, and the dragon's body humped that way. Yeah, it's nice, but don't you think he dominates the center too much with his head? He dominates St. George too much."

She would never understand. This goody-goody fanatical egotist of a mad saint had tormented some poor dragon out of his barrow and, in an unparalleled example of savage conceit, threatened to kill him. Obviously the dragon had tolerated all he could. I mused on the limitations of the art. I could not show all this in a painting, stuck as it is in its own single moment of time and space. Lessing was right about the arts.

I tried another tack: "What do you think of the dragon?"

"Oh, he's okay, yeah, he's nicely done. But—well, he's

not really scary enough. Shouldn't he vomit poison or something and——"

"We don't do that."

"Oh, I'm sorry. Now you're mad at me. I mean, well, it's really a groovy dragon. I—I just keep forgetting you're real, and——"

She didn't have to go on. I understood well enough the species gap. For a human being to learn something, it seems necessary for him to forget something that he has already been taught. A very mysterious procedure to us. But I am only speculating, since we can learn and we forget nothing. For instance, I would not forget that her attitude toward the picture expressed where her final allegiance must lie. Can man learn resistance to his own destruction, a destruction that would come about through the achievement of desire? As I write this I fear that the answer is no. My vision is of Lilith staring at the chest of balm.

But to go on. The two chests remained in their alcoves, and in the one harboring the chest of balm there was the painting of Gwynfyd. The chest was in a corner covered casually with an old Indian blanket. Gwynfyd's portrait faced the entrance.

I could tell she liked it. She gazed at it in the way she had looked up into the trees for the mockingbird. I was pleased. "That's your dragoness, isn't it?" she said. "She's beautiful. Why, she's all blue with gold tints. She's like a chameleon, sorta." I had depicted Gwynfyd in profile grazing in an orchard. Her golden tongue was flickering out to reach for an apple above her head. She had not reared herself on hind legs but stood on one tipclaw with the other foreclaw raised slightly from the ground. It was a most delicate pose and caught Gwynfyd's natural grace. In the

sky was Sun. Earth lay green, golden, and alive. I had always been very pleased with the painting.

I watched Lilith unconsciously arch her feet and stand
almost on tiptoe, then slowly relax again. I was amused.
For a moment she had wished to be a supremely beautiful
blue-and-gold-tinted dragoness with a flickering tongue
grazing in an apple orchard. The *Blerwm* says that if we
hadn't existed human beings would have imagined us.
They would have made us other and better than themselves in order to satisfy their longing to become whatever
their minds could conjure. I must admit that Lilith standing there on tiptoe, wide-eyed, and pretty kept me from
sarcasm as I had these thoughts. Indeed, I was reminded
of the charm of human creatures—most charming in the
expression of their desires. But most dangerous, too.

I had known all that. The point was that, having taken
this human waif into the barrow, I could not leave her to
come upon the remaining chests alone. I had already taken
too great a chance with her when the humanosophers appeared. So my strategy must be to impress upon her the
necessity of care with the chests, rather than let her blun-
der upon them in ignorance. The balm was particularly
tantalizing, even aside from its beckoning mystery, for it
was of attractive odor, and these California girls no doubt
loved to rub smelly suntan lotion all over themselves. At
least television certainly indicated that it was a groovy experience. [Here there is a pause in the tape. ED.] Well, I
did it, didn't I? I suppose we are collectors of words, too.

While Lilith was still admiring the picture, moving up
close to it and observing the brushmanship and the detail,
I removed the blanket from the chest. She turned quickly,
as if startled by a loud noise. Her expression was one of as-

tonishment. She stared at the chest, then at me. My eyes were a very deep purple, the triangles on my back erect, my tail flexed. She had learned soon enough that when the eyes turn purple the dragon means business.

"You frighten me," she whispered. "I have never seen your eyes quite like that."

"Yes. I mean for you to be frightened. If you are to be in these halls you must know there are great dangers in what I guard. You must never come here alone; you must never investigate this chest or the other one. Or drink from any chalice here. No matter how thirsty, no matter how curious."

"What would you do if I did?" she teased. I must say that she had nerve when it counted, for she seemed to have relaxed. The teasing was ominous. It expressed a certain resentment and lust. It stubbornly missed the point.

"If you were to do what I have warned against it would be too late for me to help you," I explained quietly, easing the darkness of my eyes. I did not like the look on her face of human female acquisitive shrewdness, the same look I had observed on the face of the Santa Barbara girl long ago and more recently on quiz and giveaway shows. She stared at that box as if she wished to seduce it. She was transfixed. Then as I turned to throw the blanket back over the chest she came to my side, reached to my neck just behind my ears, and scratched me there very softly. This makes the dragon's ears rise up, not quite rigidly as when we are on the alert, but in a somewhat less vertical fashion. This she liked, and she giggled.

"Dragon," she said, "I really like you. I like your eeeeeeears." I haunched myself and surrounded her with my tail while she stroked my ears. They are of very soft leather like suede, and of a light green on the outside, of chartreuse-yellow inside. I suspected her of considering their value on the market, then arranged the thought in a back room of my brain. "Dragon," she said huskily, "you've told me more than you meant to, haven't you? But you can trust me. I won't tell anyone anything, nothing, never," and she stroked my ears and scratched right where my neck meets the skull. It does something to us, all right. How she knew this I don't know, except that I suppose it is a sort of instinct with them. Then she stood before me with her arms about my neck, scratching it slowly with both hands. Of course, I wished to grasp her with both claws and with the tail simultaneously. Of course, I was ready to carry her from the alcove to my favorite lair in the Great Hall. But I remained rigidly composed and *Geis*-restrained. I had erred enough already. I waited. If one's ears are being stroked, one expects a price to be exacted.

"Dragon," she said, "I—I—I wonder if you——"

"You wonder if I will tell you what's in the chest." I sighed.

"Well, I mean there's no harm in it. After all, I know it's here and I might as well understand what it's all about, and——"

"I know, I know." And I did know. I knew it was inevitable that she would ask, and her argument was sound, I suppose. The question reduced itself to whether ignorance or partial knowledge is better. I believe some human poet gave his answer to this question, and came down on the side of ignorance. Maybe he was fallible, maybe prophetic. We shall see. I could not turn back now, for her ignorance was no longer pure.

"Well, all right," I said, "but you must be careful, and you must above all *believe* me."

"Oh, I always believe you. Why," she said, laughing, "I even believe *in* you!"

"All right." I knew she had me. "Do you remember the myth of King Midas and the gold and how his wish finally destroyed him?"

"Yeah, I guess so, he's the cat that wanted everything he touched to turn to gold, and everything did."

"Yes, well, I want you to remember that. Remember that the things we are about to discuss are dangerous."

"Yeah, well he was sorta stupid. I mean he could have made a wish that would have got him out of that corner. Like, saying it's only when I snap my fingers I want things to turn to gold. I mean he just wasn't very smart."

"True, but the myth is supposed to be a warning that *no one* is ever that smart. No people, anyway."

"You dragons are *very superior types,* aren't you?" she said with a touch of sarcasm.

"That's for you to decide." She was silent. Score one.

After a suitable pause I continued. "You remember the business about Pygmalion and Galatea, don't you?"

"Who? What?"

I resisted a homiletic on the virtues of classical education and the study of mythology, which though all mixed up is so important to man, being the closest confusion in his education to the ultimate songs of pythonosophy.

"Well, Pygmalion was the sculptor who made a beautiful statue of a woman and fell in love with her. Aphrodite turned her into a human being, and he married her, or so the story goes in human myth."

"So?"

"Well, human beings get a lot of things backwards. At

the least they should have gone on with the tale and described how imperfect she turned out to be." Imperfectly
beautiful, I thought. I looked at Lilith. She had a slight,
very slight scar above her right eyebrow. Her nose turned
up a little bit too much perhaps. No, she was not Galatea.
But she was what she was. And the scar and the nose were
part of it.

"Do you dragons have a story like that?"

"About human beings there is a prophecy. No, we
don't have any stories like that about us."

"What's the prophecy?"

"It's hard to tell it." Before I gave everything away at
least I thought I should be coaxed, maybe have my neck
scratched and ears stroked.

She did, and I told.

"The prophecy in the *Blerwm* is a warning against perfect beauty. It says to people, stay away, or don't look outward, make it from what you have." Beauty is cold, says
Knäckerune. "It also says beware of those who would offer
it."

She eyed the chest again. She had ceased to caress my
suede ears. She advanced her hand toward the blanket and
patted the chest through it.

"You mustn't," I said, and my eyes turned darkest purple. "You must *never* touch it."

Her eyes glittered, they really did. She looked at me,
at the chest, then at me. Her eyes glittered at me, but not
for me or the softness of my ears. She was breathing heavily, as in a sort of passion. "Oh, Dragon," she said. "Oh, oh,
how awful," and she knelt beside me with her head on my
shoulder, and she cried. She sobbed, and her cheek was
damp against my leathery pelt.

She did not look at the chest, only at Gwynfyd's portrait, and as we left the alcove, she said again, "She is beautiful." There was sadness in the way she said it. But she was right, of course. Only dragons can be beautiful and live.

Now I must make an apology. I realize that this account has somehow become more the truth about Lilith than the truth about dragons, but the truth about dragons is, you see, hopelessly entwined with the truth about man.

March 27

That was only the beginning of the night's adventure with Lilith. When she first came I had sensed that she was moody. The thing with the humanosophers had gotten to her, and now there was the depressing business of the chest. But I suspected that there was more. We were in the Outer Hall and she reclined in the corner and stared at the ceiling for a long time while I cleaned things up a bit about the house. Finally I too lay down, watching her.

"There's something I haven't told you," she said after I had stared her into speaking.

"I thought so," I replied.

"You did?"

"Yes, something bothered you from the moment you came up here this time."

"Yeah, well, it's Bobby." My eyes darkened. "He wonders where I'm going. I think he followed me once, maybe. I joked about going to see the dragon again. I mean I *really* joked, but I'm not sure he doesn't suspect something, because, well, you see, I'm not acting quite the same probably, and he can tell that, and besides I've tried to avoid him."

"Oh," I replied somewhat archly.

"I know what you're thinking. I mean me going around with a motorcycle nut or something."

"I didn't say anything."

"Yes, you did, you said 'Oh.'"

This girl was all right, I thought. But I didn't want it left there. It was important to know whether Bobby was going to appear here soon. But the issue with her was herself, and the fact that Bobby was probably sneaking around trying to find out what *she* was doing. She *didn't like that.* She was annoyed. In fact, part of Lilith is annoyed that she has let herself get involved with Bobby in the first place, because in truth she hates motorcycles and Bobby's pals. And besides, he's on narcotics some of the time, and she doesn't really like that and doesn't want to get hooked herself. In short, she's someone else and doesn't want to be whatever Bobby's existence implies. Strange, these poor *Wyrd*less creatures, seeking to find out why they are.

It is clear that I am learning in experience what I already knew in theory, that the media are not going to tell us dragons what it's really like to live in human society. Because it's very much more complicated than you can imagine from TV. Oh, there's the crime and all the social problems and the danger and the violence. That's all there. But what goes on inside them while all those things are happening outside, why, TV hasn't gotten anywhere near that yet. I see what Lilith's problem is, really. This girl is a pretty smart, rather independent-minded creature with things to say and maybe a sharp tongue, and she doesn't want to sit behind Bobby on a motorcycle the rest of her life. Yet she has this thing about Bobby, I guess.

"I didn't mean to give away anything," she said. "I mean Bobby and I started joking about the dragon as a sort of other boyfriend to me, or whatever a dragon is, and when he'd go off to work at the shop, he'd joke at me about whether the dragon was going to call, that he'd be coming back for lunch maybe."

"You're living with him." I didn't like the idea of it.

"Well, yeah, I mean yeah off and on. Off right now. Hey, Dragon, you jealous or something? Your eyes just turned green."

I laughed and smoked up the ceiling. It was a cheap trick, but I had to do something. I guess I was jealous.

She thought it was just great, the laughing, but I hadn't fooled her. She had scored a point against me in this human game we were playing. In any case, Lilith was upset because as the joke about her and the dragon developed it ceased to be quite a joke and became a sort of reality, or at least a confusion.

"It was as if, well, I mean, it was as if you really existed."

"Don't I?"

"I—I don't know sometimes. When I get back there it's as if you don't and I made you up to protect me or something, because I keep using you in that role. That's funny, isn't it—making you a protector of people when all the stories have us fighting you or something?"

"Not so strange," I said. "You may know a dragon better than any of those storytellers ever did."

"Yeah, if you're real, I mean, like the dragons they tell about."

There was nothing for me to say.

"Bobby isn't any genius. I mean he couldn't think up a thing like this, but he has an idea like I've made you real, somehow. Like you're real to me now, or a crazy obsession inside me, and he hates you. I don't know, sometimes with the drugs and all, I think he gets reality and fantasy mixed up."

"But in either case, he'd be mistaken if he thought I wasn't real, wouldn't he?"

"Oh, God . . ."

"Well, I am a real dragon. I suppose I could be an obsession, too." It is a good thing that dragons cannot leer, for I probably would have tried it at this point.

"Oh God, yes, I know, but when I get back there and we play this silly game of my having seen the dragon, why then you aren't real. I mean I'm lying while I'm telling the truth. I hate it. I really ought to tell him the dragon is really real so that I could be telling him the truth. It's not right making a fiction out of a real mythological beast, if you see what I mean. But now that we have this game going and we pretend the dragon is real, there's no way of agreeing that it really is."

"And so you are just watching each other, and he's growing suspicious."

"Yeah, and I think he's going to tell others. I mean so far it's been between us, but if he's suspicious he'll bring along his riding friends, and they'll all be up here tormenting you."

"Like the Geats," I thought aloud.

"What?"

"Oh, nothing, it's not a unique situation—a bunch of people being gotten together to attack something they don't believe in, only to find it's real."

She took this in the allegorical sense and nodded

sagely. There were times in our relationship when I guess she thought I was being very profound and speaking in riddles or Delphic utterances. She is actually better educated than I had first thought her. She seems to have read a lot, and a lot of it seems to have been romances. I suppose that she is a Tolkien bug.

Right now, however, her mind was on Bobby. "Y'know, he doesn't really think much, but he has sorta the right instincts, like he's really kind to me, and it isn't as if he was some Hell's Angel or anything. I mean it's just that he loves machinery and putting together old cars and fixing up stuff. Y'know he'd like those cars you've got. If you two went into partnership you could really do some real good things with old cars. He with the engines, I mean." But then her tone changed, and she seemed detached. "But even if he is a great lover and I get this passionate feeling and all that, and even if he wants to travel all over the place and—still what's the use of going someplace and not seeing it or learning about it, or——"

She was simply talking in, around, and to herself now, in love with her own deeper spirituality, reining in her affection. As she overflowed with spirit and pure idea, she somehow revealed herself as more completely hedonistic than her body's presence could make me feel. There was something cloying and sexual in her obeisance to spirit. It must be something about the sunlight in these parts. I don't know.

I did realize, though, that I was turning her into an object of analysis, wondering what *it* was going to do next, or say next.

"Well, to make a long story short, with the drugs and our playing this game and Bobby in love with me, I think he isn't separating truth from fiction, and he's coming up here one of these days for sure, hell, maybe today," and she lay back on the pillows and laughed and laughed: "Can't separate truth from fiction, can't separate truth from fiction, hahahaha, hahahahahahahahaha." Actually, though, there were tears streaming down her face.

March 28

This is an essay on the dragon's compulsion. I return to the subject now because I have just experienced it, known it again, and in the midst of my most crucial work. Human beings also fall victim to compulsions, the variety of which must be immense, for surely no beast surpasses the human being for perverse inventiveness. Our compulsion I have already mentioned. It is our only one, beyond our annual rage, and does not seem susceptible to therapy, exorcism, or acts of will. It is the yang that goes with our yin. I do not call it the evil that accompanies our good, because I cannot even conceive of our good without the "evil," and the term is thus inappropriate. It is the other side of our good. We collect because we are the finest of guards, or we are the finest of guards because we collect. One may take one's choice of these two propositions, but I suspect, as the *Blerwm* says in one of Knäckerune's most philosophical moments, that the two propositions are really one truth that we can't quite get into a single verbal assertion. When the urge to collect comes upon us, we can delay it for a few days or hours, but it will have its way.

Last night it had its way. I knew it was coming, and

what a terrible time for it to appear! After all, I had to deal with Lilith, who was still in the Hall and showed no sign of leaving on her own. I would like to have trusted her to remain where she had slept and not go back to investigate the chests. Yet I could not allow her to accompany me. It would be far too dangerous should she be seen, and I would be moving much faster than on a simple stroll, which was too fast even for a well-conditioned girl like Lilith. The human stories of dragons ravaging the countryside provide some sense of how fast we can travel. By human standards we move with tremendous speed, and we climb with agility. I shall not say that the dragon at his greatest velocity is a thing of beauty. He does not glide over the ground. He moves with bursts of energy that carry him in hops or lopes, using his wing-fins to help propel him into the air and back down to Earth in huge arcs. He can spring. At slower rates he scurries. Wing-fins are kept close to the body in this case, and the tail is always held out straight to provide a sort of rudder. Especially in the young dragon, tail control on land is something to be learned, and to be learned well and soon. It comes naturally to the child in the water of the tarn, but the scurry and the rushing lope require alert muscular control of the tail, for if the tail begins to wave even during a scurry, the dragon tends to follow a meandering course. Should this continue for any length of time one of two things occurs: either the dragon becomes somewhat landsick or the waving of the tail turns into an awkward flapping and he is in danger of serious accident. He is out of control. My brother Killaraus cartwheeled spectacularly into a large Oak near Corrib when he was about sixty-five and suffered several cracked vertebrae and a chipped diamond. It is strange. In the water the tiniest dragon instinctively knows how to control his tail.

But to return to my subject. As I have said, when the collecting compulsion comes upon a dragon he may delay but not overcome the powerful urge. With me it began this way: When Lilith ran her hands over the stately chassis of the old Marmon, I felt a familiar prickling along the row of triangles that crown my back. The feeling begins in the uttermost tail-triangle and moves slowly to the base of the neck. The process can be slowed considerably by immersing oneself at once in a cool tarn, but it is irreversible and will eventually arrive at the head and make its demand of the brain. With Lilith deep in the barrow I could hardly rush out for a dip, but I did amble over to my underground stream and take a long, cool drink. This didn't reveal anything to Lilith, and I felt that I had managed to delay things a few hours—that at the worst I could get Lilith bedded down and asleep before I set out. At best I might induce her to return whence she had come. It is strange. I knew very few facts about Lilith. I had no idea where she lived or what she did most of the time.

You can imagine my agitation, for, as you know, she was pressing to see more and more. This was one of the reasons that I turned the conversation to Bobby, simply to keep her away from any greater knowledge. Ah, it was a very bad time for the compulsion to present itself at the tip of my tail.

But Lilith had already decided to return to town that night, because she had an engagement. It hadn't been necessary to insinuate my serpentlike suggestion that she go back to ease Bobby's suspicions. I was free to act. The compulsion had reached the base of my tail by now. I gave in to it and it raced up my back, stinging my spine, and invaded my brain. It was a powerful force. I lay stunned on the barrow floor, and there flew across the Cinerama of my mind a shower of cut-glass bottles and baubles, china plates, butter molds, and saucers, scraps of old bowls, Pyrex coffeepots, and worn knives, forks, and spoons. Then passed the old jugs, and, floating majestically, the Ultimate Model T. Finally, lo, there came upon me a great burst of strength, my head cleared of its stupendous vision, the strange sensation along my triangles subsided beginning with the tip of my tail and proceeding up to my neck. It is a curious feeling of relief, but actually it is only the rolling up of the whole compulsion into the brain. The result is an intensification of the sense perceptions and a feeling of extreme well-being and singleness of purpose. I experienced absolutely no anxiety over the fact that the object of my quest had not revealed itself. It would come to me in the usual way as I searched. Only as vague suggestion had it ever been known to manifest itself before then. Like *Wyrd* and *Geis*, it was discoverable only in the act. I reminded myself of one thing: the dragon tends to recklessness about manifesting himself to people during the earliest stages of the compulsion. I admit in the past to causing occasional brush fires when, careless, I have had to fall back upon some device of distraction.

I set out. At great speed I loped and arced through the ravines and hills toward Santa Barbara, all my heightened senses at the ready. I was open to the least hint about the object of my search. It was dark, but not so dark that I could move totally unnoticed unless I took care. Strange large objects that seemed like crates, railroad cars, or buses loomed in my mind as I rushed on. The town was quiet. I kept to back streets and alleys. Occasionally a dog barked. Closer in, I scurried nose to the ground through yards and along hedges. Things were becoming clearer to me. A red caboose vaguely wavered in my mind, a Greyhound bus superimposed itself upon it.

Suddenly as I turned into a wide back street I saw at mid-block a large group of people walking in my direction in a variety of outlandish dress. In the few moments before I ducked into a huge parking lot and crouched between two large black limousines, I could make out a number of strange costumes. There were girls in long, white dresses and glittering crowns, girls in abbreviated cowboy suits, girls in bikinis, in miniskirts, in tights. There were girls in drum majorette costumes familiar to me from the Game of the Week. There were young men walking about in colorful martial outfits with tall, fuzzy hats and musical instruments. Behind them I could see policemen and huge-hatted cowboys reining in their steeds. They were all coming my way in a sort of disorganized procession. Suddenly there was a voice blaring through a bullhorn somewhere behind me in the parking lot. I was startled, looked about for an escape route, saw none, and froze. The speaker was shouting complicated directions about the order of procession that seemed only to confuse people as they streamed into the lot. Some were getting into the cars. As my eyes searched the darkness I realized that many of the vehicles in the lot were in fact large, dragon-sized floats, converted automobiles, or trucks. Now the girls were giggling and shrieking and rushing through the lot to leap upon these floats. It was going to be a parade; yes, it was the Merchants' Easter Season Parade. I had seen it on the tube last year. It had included a barely adequate papier-maché dragon.

This realization came upon me just as two white-booted, miniskirted, Oriental brunettes carrying electrically illuminated batons came around the corner of the Lincoln next to me and squealed with delight, "Here's the dragon. Here's the dragon." One leapt quite suddenly onto my shoulders and offered the other a hand. Soon both stood on my back, swinging their batons, practicing their routine, I suppose. What could I do but remain absolutely still? The recklessness that accompanies our compulsion had put me in a dreadful fix.

The girls on my back were talking, now, about where Pete and Tom were. And they must have been wiggling around adjusting their costumes because I almost lost my balance what with the tension of trying to be completely rigid and, of course, the ignominy. I heard one of them say, "We're number six." "Hey, Allen," one shouted into my ear, "you know that, don't ya? We're number six."

I winced and took Allen to be the operator of me, so I answered, muffling my voice appropriately, "Yeah, okay baby, we're number six, just hang on when this thing flies." Because I now realized that, surrounded as I was by floats and cars in the lot, like it or not I was going to be in the parade. And sure enough, number six was called sixth, and I crept out toward the driveway following a big Cadillac disguised as a forest with Smokey the Bear walking around above it and a dark-haired girl with a gold crown and a long, white evening dress beside him. When she turned around I saw it was Lilith.

It was more of a shock to her than to me. She shrieked, but no one including Smokey himself, who inside his costume was apparently someone named Jack, took any notice, since everyone else seemed to be shrieking, too. She hurried to the end of her float and bent down to my low creeping form.

"Firedrake, baby, for chrissakes, what're you doing here? It's you, isn't it? Have you lost your mind?"

"I'm trapped," I pleaded. "Help me get rid of these dolls. They just hopped right on me. There's gotta be a real dragon float somewhere in the lot. Number six," I added feebly. I was a pathetic sight.

"A real dragon float," she laughed. I could have throttled her. If she didn't do something quickly those two idiot girls would prance all over me through downtown Santa Barbara, and surely there'd be someone in the crowd with the imagination to see a real dragon.

Lilith was standing straight up looking around the lot now, and in a moment she spotted the missing float. "Hey, Jo, Lea, I think you've got the wrong dragon float. You're number six, aren't you? It's over there, over in the corner. This is twelve."

The two girls, who had been tromping all over me in their boots, facing each other and shouting out numbers or rhythms or something, finally got the word and they hustled down off me, shouting thanks to Lilith and running with their quite nice rear ends bobbing under their skirts in the general direction Lilith had pointed. But it was too late not to be swept up in the parade, and I was riderless. So Lilith excused herself for a moment from Smokey the Bear and hopped lithely, considering she wore a long dress, up on my shoulder, saying, "Look, like just keep going right straight on, and as soon as we find a convenient street or alley, well, you go on down it. I'll hop off then and get back on the float ahead. This parade won't be moving very fast for a while."

And so, very stately with funereal gait, I moved toward the parking-lot entrance. As we passed into the street, one child on the corner stared dumbfounded at me, pointed, and shouted, "Mommy, Daddy, there's a dragon. Look, a real dragon." And the parents smiled indulgently down on the child and pointed out Smokey the Bear. Farther along the block the daddies watched Lilith, in her low-cut, white, clinging dress, and I was merely her steed. Miss Keep California Green for 1970. "What would Smokey think if he only knew?" I whispered to her.

"Oh, shut up," she said, smiling and waving, I supposed. "Look for an alley," and she gouged me at the base of my skull. I wanted to laugh. In truth, it was a desperate situation. The object of my compulsion was supposed to be formulating itself in the depths of my mind, and now I had to concentrate on how to escape from this ridiculous parade. Somewhere behind us a high-school band struck up a slow lugubrious version of "Come On, Baby, Light My Fire," and everyone clapped. When she regained her composure, Lilith leaned down to one ear and said that if I was gonna be in this parade then I'd better start marching along or gliding like a station wagon but not lope or roll from side to side like a drunk. It was making her sick. "Yes, indeed," I replied, and did what I could to move at an awkwardly human pace. In truth, Lilith and I managed a whole block and a half of sparse crowds before the opportunity to turn off came. And when we did fall out of line, one of the fuzz motorcycled up to the curb where we'd parked and said, "Hey, Lil, anything wrong?" The very sound of a motorcycle raised all my triangles, but Lilith said I should remain calm, and she sent old Rodney off on his steed after explaining we'd get back in line in a minute, there was something Otto was fixing underneath. The fuzz varoomed away, and Lilith leaped off me, with a blown kiss of good-by, and vaulted athletically onto the

Smokey Bear float, just as the parade really started moving, turning on to the main drag of Santa Barbara. I relaxed at the curb for a moment, then I made a passable imitation of starting an engine, backed up, swung my rear out toward the traffic of the parade, obstructing the march of two drum majors, one of whose batons gave me a bad crack on the spine, and drove myself slowly and smoothly down a long alleyway between two buildings. In the darkness I rested, a buzz of sensation around me. I saw that I was heading in the direction of the municipal bus park, at the end of the alley. Those great metal beasts I contemplated with considerable relief. I went among them, and we all stood silently as if settled for the night or grazing quietly in some asphalt meadow. I rested again. I was rather tired, there was no one about, and it seemed that I would be safe for a while.

In relative quiet the compulsion began slowly to clarify itself. It was as if my presence among the buses aided me in discovering the object. For there now floated before me, superimposed one upon another, the visions of a caboose, a summer cabin, and one of my big soot-snorting colleagues. I recognized suddenly that the object of my search was the Ultimate Mobile Home, to be drawn like my Model T from the scavengings of many dumps, collected piecemeal from construction sites, from disposal areas, and perhaps from mobile-home villages themselves. It was clear that I could not count on assembling a complete example of a mobile home from things discarded. I could see it now. I would furnish it with contemporary works of art, overstuffed chairs heavily spray-lacquered in brilliant colors. (I could only tolerate useless chairs.) My compulsion would ebb and flow, of course. But it would return ever, until the exhibit was complete, until I had made art from the meaningless productivity and consequently tasteless trash of man.

My strength renewed, I looked about me and planned my activities for the remainder of the evening. I would reconnoiter. I would find some typical examples of mobile homes near to hand, preferably on the edge of the city, proximate to my line of retreat back to the hills. I scurried, slunk, and wandered through alleys and down dark streets. I systematically maneuvered past houses and shopping areas. Occasionally a wandering dog would come upon me, his ferocity drained as he apprehended my size and impressive demeanor. I wandered through Santa Barbara for what must have been two hours, and my journey took me farther from the center of town, where I had so recklessly exposed myself.

The mobile homes that struck my fancy were grouped in a circular Indianlike enclave in a small canyon that had a stream threading through it. It was 12:00 p.m. by human reckoning when I came upon them, and almost all of the twenty or thirty units were dark. Beside each was its Detroit steed-of-steel. Behind each a picnic table, a washline strung, a barbecue. I observed the whole setting from a rise to its north. Slowly I came down, sniffing the atmosphere like a huge dog, for when we are compelled our sense of smell is the most intensified of all. Something smelled familiar and not far away but also not quite clear. I crept the last few yards toward a home with fake board-and-batten walls. The smell came stronger now, and I recognized it at last as the peculiar waft of a motorcycle. There it was in the darkness, settled against one wall of the house. Nearer, I recognized that the wall had been dented in a number of places, and the paint was chipping. The motorcycle was a Yamaha.

I proceeded past a heap of old beer cartons and cases and, beyond that, a large birdbath with a ceramic flamingo leaning against it. I thought a moment about these objects. Their aesthetic potential was slight, of course, but they were a part of cultural history. Nevertheless, I passed them by. I wished to begin the assembly of my mobile home this night. I circled the building. For my initial foray any loose objects would suffice. Reconnaissance was the main objective at this stage.

But the wretched thing seemed all of one piece, or made so by rivets. As I cautiously peered around the last corner another smell came upon me, rather like peppermint. The window on this last wall was open about six inches, the shade drawn up to that height. Inside the room the light flickered like a candle. I could hear the murmuring of a quiet conversation, moving in fits and starts. I knew that the Yamaha was Bobby's, and that one of the voices had to be Lilith's. I worried about being seen from the dirt road that ran in front of the curved row of these strange and vulgar edifices, but I was overcome by curiosity. Auburn my eyes, had there been light for anyone to see. I crept to the window, and pressed my eyes to the small opening.

The dragon is a fastidiously neat creature. It is a good thing, too, what with our collecting compulsion. Otherwise our barrows would look like the worst sorts of junk yards. What I first observed seemed to be a great mass of debris. The room was filled with parts and pieces of machines. In one corner was a large worktable on which were a number of old radios and a couple of small television sets in various states of dissection. Everywhere there were old fenders and headlights, parts of engines, and tools. It appeared that a motorcycle had been completely stripped in the room.

But that is not all that was stripped, for Bobby reclined naked in a bulbous overstuffed chair, a huge striped towel flung across his body. Lilith lolled on a daybed in one corner under a blanket; all of her that showed, her head and shoulders, was bare. Her white dress was hung on a wall picture-hanger. She wore her crown at a rakish angle. She seemed to be looking at a magazine, but could not have been reading it, for it was too dark. I had been right; only a candle provided flickering illumination. For the moment they were silent, and I thought that they had heard me sidle up and were listening, but I was wrong. Bobby was leaning back staring at the ceiling where shadows danced with the flame.

Lilith looked up from the magazine. "Okay, so I'm back," she said. "For a time; don't make a big thing out of it."

"I made *you*, baby, Miss Queen." He took the towel and swung it in the air in a huge circle, tried to make it snap. It didn't, and he relaxed back into the chair.

"Haha," she replied sarcastically.

"Well, yeah, haha, I suppose. It was fun. I guess your dragon doesn't take very good care of your needs, does he? I mean youall having to come around here to get laid."

"Don't be a snot."

"Hey, Lil, how does a dragon do it, I mean without squashing you or burning you up?"

I was outraged. The idea of such a conversation! After my exemplary behavior! Then I reminded myself of the game they were playing. And that they weren't talking about me.

Except that they really were! I wondered how long it could remain a game. Bobby was serious and bitter beneath his joking.

"This dragon thing is getting to be a bore," Lilith said in a flat voice, and picked up a piece of celery from a big plate of stalks and carrots. She chewed it and turned the pages of the magazine. She lay on her stomach, her head propped on one elbow. I observed the outline of the very satisfactory rest of her under the blanket, which had slipped from her shoulders now. She was a remarkably acceptable human female, indeed. All of her.

"Okay, so why did you start it, or does everything get to be a bore with you? That seems to be it, doesn't it, baby? You just wear it out." He was observing a sparkplug, holding it up as if offering a toast. "I guess I'm not very smart or whatyoucallit . . ."

"Verbal."

". . . but some things get through to me. That dragon business just protects the hell out of you. Like you can live that fantasy world any time things get too real, can't ya? Hey, did y'ever hear the one about the duchess and the bull?"

"Yeah," said Lilith, chomping on celery. "Yeah, don't tell it."

"Look, Lilith, you just . . ."

She turned toward him, lying now on her side with her head on her fist. A lot of her showed, and a lot of her anger too. "Look, so you think the dragon business is a fantasy. What about your motorcycle and all this crap strewn around here? You just get right inside this stuff and

128

hide in it, don't you? Any time the idea of thinking comes
up. Any time you might get involved. Any time maybe
some idea is about to violate you."

That impressed me as rather original until I remembered it was Eliot's phrase. Then I was impressed at Lilith,
using Eliot, who was like pretty ancient. And then it
seemed strange, her lying there in the middle of all that
machinery with a jockey. Well, the *Blerwm* never pre-
tended that human beings were not mysterious.

They were getting along famously, each accusing the
other of escapism. Observing the decor, I thought I'd want
to break that jail myself. But of course I was putting the
dragon view on the mess the room was in. On the other
hand, Bobby had proved to be a bit of a collector, and I
couldn't ignore that he had some nice automotive items in
there. Old Bobby didn't seem to me such a hopeless fellow
after all. There's got to be some good in every collector.

"I started to say——" he said.

"When you were so rudely interrupted," Lilith droned
in a bored voice. Bobby wadded up his towel and heaved
it into a corner. He glared at her.

"I started to say *to myself* that she's a hopeless bitch.
She's arrogant, she's self-centered, she wants to be able to
hold something over everybody." He leaped up and
hopped across the room. One foot seemed to be sore or
something. He landed beside her on the daybed, saying,
"But she's a damned good piece of ass."

She turned on her back, and he put his arm under her
head. "Oh, Bobby," she said, "why don't you stop ducking
out on your horse and get committed?"

"To what? The Friendly Loan Company? The U.S.
Marines? My Winston?"

"You know that's not what I mean. I mean to some

ideal, to what's going on. Like there's all these problems and——"

"Why don't you stop running away from me?" he interrupted, and kissed her. Then they were both under the blanket, and she said, "Look, Bobby, I mean——"

"I'm not looking, I'm feeling." And she laughed, a laugh I hadn't heard before, but I wondered whether she wasn't crying a little bit inside, because she was really arrogant and suspected she had it in her to be something, if she could find out what that something was. And maybe old Bobby, maybe he did have somewhere to go.

Who invented the awful rules of the human game of discovery? Who insisted on working in the anxiety? I thought of what the two of them lived in right now. A building you pick up and put on wheels and send anywhere. But where?

"Look, baby," he went on, after they were serious again, "I'm not running away from anything. I'm running right at you right now. That's all there is. That's all there is. That's all——"

And then there wasn't any talking.

I turned from the window and haunched nearby. I stared up at the hills from which I had come. The sky was fairly clear and there were some stars. Solitude and simplicity invited me. I was disappointed. Disappointed in Lilith, because in truth it seemed foolish of her to have gone back to Bobby. It was a sort of failure, especially after having approached so close to the treasure. After all, she knew more now by immediate experience than most human beings would ever know through wisdom. Maybe it was attaining some sense of her own incompleteness that troubled her. Her experience with me had thus worked in reverse, and she would settle for riding the motorcycle to nowhere now in a sort of nihilistic madness. No, she had been bitten by the possibility of knowledge or complete experience or however she was able to put it to herself. She had stood before that chest, and she could never forget that it was there. I must remember that.

Strangely enough, it was Bobby who was complete. He wasn't buying that commitment rhetoric. He might motor-cycle to nowhere, or linger on as a mechanic in some two-bit chiseler's garage, and then maybe own his own some-time, and he'd be absolutely honest and never make any money to speak of. He'd fix a lot of cars and be thought a sort of genius by the lawyers and professors and business-men who brought their transmission problems to him and sometimes would hang around watching him work at the last few things on the job. Through it all he'd grow more separate and think even less. That would be after he'd traveled all over the place on his chopper, after he'd given up the club, unrolled his sleeping bag in some relatively permanent place. The whole point of thoughtlessness may be to banish the idea of a dragon's Hoard. Maybe that was human sanity.

Lilith would never buy it. Whether the dragon was real or not (and I supposed she really did come back from the hills and decide I wasn't there at all and then have to come back up to confirm the whole thing), she had seen it in her mind, and it would never be exorcised.

That was what their destiny should have been, accord-ing to the rules as I understood them. But somehow I doubted the rules applied here. I was a new wild card. Be-cause though Bobby hadn't worked it out, something closer to the truth of what had happened to Lilith was going to appear to him. It would be in *his* terms when it came, for Bobby *was* someone. She tormented him for being it. She wanted to prove she was superior, or that she had the power to change what she really didn't like. But she was tied to him in a primitive sort of way typical of young love.

Enough, I thought. It was too human. I was thinking into their bodies. I was becoming them. Bad. Besides, at this moment, I heard them talking:

"You still think there's someone else I'm seeing." I knew it. She really couldn't let the whole thing go. She would play with him.

"Nah, I guess not." He was silent for a while, and then he said, "But you go off alone. Maybe I'd dig it if you went off with someone else. The alone bit is spooky. Maybe you ought to be going off to someone else. Like it's more natural."

She didn't appreciate that. "Well, I'm not doing anything of the kind. I just go where I go alone, and that's the way it is. I'm me, and I'm gonna stay me."

"Yeah, well, okay, so it's okay. Maybe I'll grab on to it sometime." He was drinking a can of beer now, draining it. She watched him impassively.

"Hey, look, Lil, there isn't anything else anywhere. I mean dammit to hell there isn't even hell. There's just this, and messing around and maybe making cars out of the spare parts that turn up. And there's getting *out* sometimes. In the woods or up north on the chopper. That's all there is."

But Lilith was staring right at the window through which I watched, staring as if she could see my eyes looking in. Her face was cold, set.

"There is something else," she said. Her eyes seemed to stare directly into mine, hidden in the darkness.

Bobby got up and began to search around for his

clothes. Lilith sat there staring. I turned away. Strange what had come over me. I had never known it to happen before. I no longer had any interest in the mobile home or any part of it. The compulsion to collect was completely absent. However, I was not without emotion. I was, in fact, annoyed, mostly at humankind. As I rounded the corner of the movable metal monstrosity, angered at it, I swung my tail and gave it a solid thwack. A stupid thing to have done.

"Gawd t'Jesus, what was *that?*" I heard Bobby shout.

Scurrying around the corner, I noticed the old bird-bath again. I took it up in one claw and disappeared into the darkness, just as the lights shot on at the neighbors' and Bobby, wrestling with his jeans, flung open a screen door.

Evening, March 29

It has been very quiet here all day. While I worked transporting the next-to-last chest through the tunnels, I fell into pondering upon the evening of my compulsion. In the drudgery of carrying these heavy objects one falls into a sort of metronomic gait. Thoughts detach themselves from the work at hand and float aimlessly. One lives, as it were, in a mental world. I began to consider whether Lilith had gone back to Bobby to protect me, to try to prove to him that there really wasn't someone up in the hills, or simply to protect her own investment in the experience. As I trudged along I decided that I wasn't up to figuring it out, and I fell into a frightening depression.

Dragon depressions are frightening because for one thing they seldom occur and are thus strange, and for another they are very unproductive. Worse, they interfere generally with vigilance. Our pleasures are not masochistic in kind, so our depressions are totally unambivalent as compared with far more complex human depressions, in which there seems to be an ingredient of pleasure bound up in despair. I felt the depression in my shoulders. It comes in the shoulders when we are carrying, the knees when we are loping, the eyes when we are staring, and so on. I did not set down the chest; I refused to submit. I knew that if I did I might be rendered rheumatoid for days, and there simply wasn't time. I also believed that part of the reason for this attack was a very unpleasant modicum of jealousy that had sprung up over Lilith's spending the night with Bobby. A blow to my pride, perhaps. A realization, too, that though she liked me, what she really was fascinated by was the treasure. Well, it was my own fault. If I hadn't exhibited all that cool restraint maybe it would have been different.

So I worked until I was quite tired and managed to complete the haul of the chest of spirit. When I returned it became clear that I should occupy myself in some way, that solitude wasn't all I thought it to be, and that the best thing was not to remain alone. So I tried to raise Feuerkugel in the northern zone.

He came in after a couple of efforts, and I was surprised to discover that he was in his rage. Now my rage always takes place during the period immediately previous to, in the midst of, and following the UCLA-USC football game. Before, because of the dreadful sports writers and other vultures; during, because of the TV blackout; and following, because of the dreadful sports writers and other vultures. The rage cannot be pleasant to observe, and the dragon's first instinct is to hide himself from all view. He is embarrassed to display his less-than-cool self before the Oaks or Earth, to say nothing of other dragons or men. I remember that my father in Corrib experienced his rage annually at Samhain. It took the form of a maddening desire to learn Irish step-dancing and a complete inability to appreciate the impossibility of this for large four-legged creatures. When it came upon him he went into the mountains of Joyce's Country for a couple of weeks, sometimes longer. He never spoke of how he occupied himself there, but my mother indicated that he simply got far away from people and tried to dance. He returned bruised about the head and tail.

My rage rarely results in physical hurt, and the exercise I get probably does me good. It expresses itself partly in a desire to write haughty, condescending letters to the Los Angeles *Times* and the *Examiner* ridiculing the sports writers and their attitude toward the BIG GAME, their ballyhoo, their second-guessing, and their complaints against the officials. I never mail the letters, though. I go outdoors and run a lot, charging directly at Oaks and then at the last minute dodging. After the rage subsides, I then must make my apologies to the Oaks. Indeed, for the rest of each year I am probably excessively courtly in my behavior toward them. I believe that they have come to accept this dragonistic eccentricity if not quite to understand it. For a while I possessed a pretty good football, but I kept puncturing it with my fangs. Though we can run holding the ball in a foreclaw, there is no doubt that we are more elusive if we hold the ball in our jaws and move on all fours.

Like my father during his rage, I practice at something I shall never be able to play. Even granting the accumulation of twenty-two dragons in one place, where could we find an adequate field?

Well, usually Feuerkugel's rage came in the late summer and fall, when he had taken all he could of the reports on the Yosemite smog and the Oregon smurk. But this year the smurk issue was getting played up in the papers early, and every time there was an article, Feuerkugel would express his outrage at the animal who can't properly employ his fires. He confessed to me once that during his rage he practiced endlessly at filling his cauldron and mouth with water and spraying it through his foreteeth, thinking to convert himself into a sort of rural fire department that could then rush about putting out the field fires that caused the smurk. And so he was going on at me about the Willamette farmers and the burning and asking what would happen if dragons behaved like that with their fire. It is a very effective question. There are millions and millions of human beings and very few dragons. Even so, if we had not adopted the most stringent breath regulations there would be a serious problem, dwarfing air pollution as man now knows it. It is said that lions do not roar in captivity with nearly the vigor that they do when free. Since the edict from Ceugant on smoke-breath, no dragon has indulged himself by bringing his full firepowers into play. In his rage Feuerkugel would finally give up on the water and consider adding so much acrid smoke to the farmers' smurk that things would be brought to a crisis. Old activist Feuerkugel. If his rage isn't given some other outlet soon, he may well break *Geis*.

No, finally he'll put first things first and leave the smurk problem to men.

I simply wanted to pass the time with Feuerkugel, and he was passing quite a lot of it with his invective. It seemed all right to tell him that I'd recently had some direct experience of human beings. This calmed him. "They are strange creatures," he said, "but I like them in person. It's in the abstract that they are so disgusting—that is, when you can start blaming the ways of the world on them, or aren't close enough to them individually to see that they are usually more decent alone." I was reminded of Bobby, and how as I heard more from him through the window I thought better of him. I had even decided that maybe the two of us could have reached some real understanding under other conditions. "But the problem is that they do herd up a lot." Then he told me of an old man who came into the hills now and then to talk with him. A crazy old man who'd been a lumberjack all over the Northwest and had commanded apple pies for breakfast in those camps in his prime. This old man, Feuerkugel went on, spent his time walking. He was retired and was supposed to be living with his daughter and son-in-law, at least he was occupying a cabin on their farm; but he just spent his time walking. That's all he did now, he just walked. He walked into town and back every weekday. He walked completely around the farm on Sundays after church. Sometimes he walked up into the hills. When he and Feuerkugel came upon each other on one of his walks, he just looked Feuerkugel in the eye and said he'd seen worse in the Republican Party and why didn't they proceed on together? So they did, and the old fellow allowed he could probably get along with any dragon as long as it wasn't running for office. They agreed about the Oregon smurk, and the old man lambasted the farmers, and the politicians in Salem, and the government, and the automobile. The old man would spit and cough and swear every other word, and Feuerkugel would listen quietly and agree sometimes or ask a question that would produce another artistic string of expletives. At the end of these walks the ranting old man would suddenly become quiet and almost courtly. He would bid the dragon good-day with a doffing of his cap and would say something to the effect that he very much enjoyed speaking with someone who really understood life, and would think about everything Feuerkugel had said, and then he would go on his way back to the farm whistling and singing dreadfully out of key. Of course, Feuerkugel hadn't said anything to speak of, and the old man had said a great deal. It didn't matter, and it didn't matter to the old man what a huge colorful dragon was doing in the hills, how he lived, what he ate, or what he guarded. Never once did the old man ask Feuerkugel any of those standard questions. They were just out on a long walk together. They were out on a walk discussing the state of things. And the old man wasn't going to do anything about anything, not any longer anyway. But he could rant. He had almost reached a dragon's understanding of rage.

Feuerkugel was telling me this because I had brought up human beings and a week ago the old man had died. It was in the paper. And maybe this was the reason that Feuerkugel was so angry about the smurk, or apparently about the smurk. It's also one of the reasons taking up with human beings is not really a very good thing for dragons. Human beings just don't live long enough. Why that old man had only lived about seventy-five years!

Feuerkugel had little to say about my report on Lilith

and Bobby, old subtle Feuerkugel. He simply asked how the moving of the treasure was going, implying that I'd better keep at it. Indeed, it hadn't been going badly, especially after getting the Quirks and Leers into their new places and enjoying peace and quiet while I was working. The new halls were a potential aesthetic improvement over the old, except for the loss of Gwynfyd's picture. It was painted right on a wall specially prepared for fresco, and there was no way to move it. I toyed with the idea of making a copy, but the whole concept offended my sensibility. Reproductions simply don't do the job.

But in all other respects the halls were well designed, and in the future I would be able to turn my leisure, if I was to have any, into productive artistry. Thus for a few moments that evening I surveyed with some satisfaction the results of my long labors, and discussed these matters with a friend.

March 30

She came back this morning. I was deep down in the alcove of the Great Hall preparing to move the last chest, the chest of balm, when suddenly she was calling through the tunnels, "Firedrake, Firedrake."

In the hazy darkness of the tunnel I could not see her well, but I knew that she was in a panic. She was hurrying toward me when I confronted her with the purpling of my eyes. I had been startled, and naturally my eyes expressed my instinct. Back in the Outer Hall, where I tried to calm her, I realized that she had been hurt, not badly perhaps, but hurt nevertheless. I suspected it was Bobby.

And it was. Oh, yes, she had gone back to him. Oh, they had gotten along all right for a while, maybe twenty-four hours, and then she started sniping at him, she was always sniping at him. Why did she do that?· (It didn't seem the time for me to offer an answer.) And after lengthy discussion and her amateur analysis of him, which led to his retaliation, they just gave up talking and rattled around in the place until he finally got out on his horse and was gone for hours. Well, as I knew, sniping talk hadn't exactly taken up their every moment, but I didn't offer this as an observation. Then when he came back he was sullen because she was in almost exactly the same damned position as when he went out, sprawled on the daybed eating celery and reading Herman Hesse. And while he paced around she just kept on eating the celery and an occasional carrot as if she were "some kind of goddamned rabbit," and paying no attention to anything except the book and maybe the carrot. Then she put the book away, finished the carrot, turned on her back, a pillow under her head, and was silent, her eyes half closed. He stood there. For all this time she was aware of him like some huge, tormenting monster. (She tactfully apologized for this remark, but smiled a bit as she did. I accepted the apology with good will.) She remained there while he gathered up his anger inside himself until she guessed he was suffering enough. But a great sadness came upon her then, and she began to cry quietly. She realized that her face was impassive.

"Get up," he said. "You can't just lie there crying."

No answer.

"Please, Lil, get up, and let's go outside, let's *get outside.*"

She had not moved or spoken. She cried.

"Okay," he said, and he came to the bed, grasped her by the arms and forced her into a standing position. She felt limp, but then gradually she stood by herself. He stepped back from her as she stood there slumped with her head bowed.

She knew what was going to happen, but she somehow accepted it or did not attempt to ward it off, maybe even wished for it. When he hit her with the palm of his hand across her face—as hard as he could—and then hit her again with the back of his hand, she felt only numbness, and she fell back upon the bed and lay there sobbing.

He stood over her, clenching and unclenching the hand he had used, holding it as if it were the hand, not she, that was hurt, and saying, "Just once, maybe, just once I've made you cry. Just once it's me and not whoever else causes it. That goddamned whoever else!"

She could not answer, but wondered what it all meant, except that she didn't really wonder what it meant because she really knew. Anyway, now she was sobbing because she was at least physically hurt, and it was sort of cleansing, almost as if Bobby had broken through in the only way it was possible.

Finally though, it was not good enough. Things were just the same, which is to say that things were not as they might be, because Bobby was finally, well, still the Bobby who loved his horse and nothing else, except her, she supposed, with all the love he could muster after the horse, and he couldn't be changed into some magnificent philosopher, or poet, or artist, or Pancho Gonzales even, or perhaps a wonderful ruby-encrusted dragon.

Then she turned to me, because she had been in the

corner speaking all of this into a handkerchief, and said, "You know, I really was crying for him, the poor slob. It's just that I don't want him to be a poor slob like he's gonna be, and like I don't wanta be with him."

"No, you were crying for yourself then, I think. Perhaps a little bit for him. Anyway, he senses the situation, but can't quite express what he somehow knows." Dear me, I thought, I'm beginning to talk in these crazy human terms.

"The Hopkins poem. It's Margaret I mourn for." Pause. "I read lots of poetry." She said this in a somewhat annoying self-congratulatory way.

I tried to ignore the tone, and added, in a somewhat self-congratulatory way, the proper lines:

> "Ah! As the heart grows older
> It will come to such sights colder."

"That's terrible, isn't it?" she said, with a sob in her voice. She was in love with her own self-pity; no, with the wonderful cloying drama of herself. Come to think of it, I had never really seen her sob before, though there had been tears on occasion. Yes, she read lots of poetry, and she made it up in her mind too, I thought. I was certainly learning something about the human ego, maybe the female ego, and the story that Grandfather told about Beowulf's women was beginning to make more sense to me. I could see those strong, ferocious creatures storming around the tarn more clearly now, brandishing their spears and shields and screaming at Eterskel. I imagine Beowulf was pleased as could be in his last moments before being done in, thinking he had drained off all that female energy and drive in the direction of a dragon hunt, when it could have been aimed at him and his throne and setting up Cerridwen again. The Druids must have stood back and stroked their beards sagely to see the women having such a grand old time of it.

Well, that's a dragon function Beowulf invented. It isn't *Wyrd,* thank heaven.

She was on her knees and looking up at me now, saying that the way Hopkins and I put it you could never cry for anyone but yourself and that wasn't fair, it wasn't a fair way to argue. Besides it just wasn't true really, because she had thought about Bobby a lot, and it was terrible. He was so beautiful outside and partly inside. There was just this one thing missing inside him, and it was because he somehow couldn't even grasp what he was missing that she was sad.

I didn't comment on Bobby as a beautiful exterior. The human male simply doesn't strike dragons as a terribly aesthetic object. In fact I didn't have much to say to her except that I thought she'd probably better get used to imperfections—surely she had some, and Bobby seemed not to mind them.

"Yeah, I suppose, but it's a question of what's really important."

I agreed.

"Maybe," I said, "you ought to think, with part of your mind, as you human beings seem to be able to do, that everything is just an adventure and that you aren't every moment making an eternal choice. Nothing has to be worldshaking all the time." I know we dragons are committed creatures and that this one thing *is* everything to us, in a sense, so I wasn't on very good ground here. That is, my advice wouldn't work for dragons at all. We define everything in the *Wyrd's* terms. Human beings with no *Wyrd* couldn't do that, and my point was that they shouldn't. In any case, that one thing couldn't be themselves. Think of a dragon, with his capacity for self-admiration, worrying about his own freedom or psyche. Why, he'd be totally impossible—worse than a *Wyrd*less human being. Maybe no dragon advice would work for human beings. I was botching things up.

So I remained silent after that, and she talked on. I began to feel somewhat bored by it. These human beings: a fundamental issue this week is just last week's news next week. A small amount of self-congratulatory *Weltschmerz* is quite enough for a dragon to endure. Our *Wyrd*, our way of life, simply eliminates ambivalence about the really fundamental issues like guarding and breath and population control.

Lilith could tell I was losing interest. Indeed, *she* was losing interest. She took a deep breath, tapped her fingers on a rock, shook her hair out, sighed, stood up, adjusted her clothing all around, moistened her lips, examined her fingernails, stretched, sat down, looked cross, and looked at me; I said nothing.

"Yeah," she said, "I've got this neurotic thing. It's a bore." She paused. "But I haven't told you the whole story," she said. "We had another argument after that. I mean he went out for a little while and came back. And it was like he was starting to get jealous all over again sorta, and he insisted I was seeing somebody else and that was what was wrong and I was a liar and a bitch who was just coming back to him when I was bored. He knew I was going up into the hills somewhere and all this business of my crying and being sullen with him only started after I'd been going away all the time. I tried to make the old joke about the dragon, and it just made him angrier. Y'know, for a moment there I thought he'd known all along about the dragon—about you, I mean. I knew he'd followed me once, and I began to wonder whether I'd really given him the slip, you know, whether he'd really seen us and was playing me out. Maybe he came around to thinking what he saw was really there that first day. Now, well, like I don't know any more."

I won't deny that this bothered me.

"Well, I—I think now he may be getting it. Oh, he's *so* dumb, sometimes. It's taken him so long to understand about the dragon, I mean about you. I'm really sorry I keep referring to you as *it.*"

I understood now that she had at least partly wanted Bobby to acknowledge there was a dragon. As for calling me *it*, that was an interesting aspect of our relationship. *It* did distance me a bit from her and make me slightly fictional. Probably she was protecting herself against me, just as she was protecting herself against Bobby. Was she protecting herself against everybody that way? Did she carry a sword and round shield?

The problem really was that every time she got bitchy with him, Bobby would disappear on his horse or get to nowhere on pot or hopped up on speed. So when it happened this time and Bobby rode off and then came back, she didn't think too much about it until it went on funny sorta. That is, Bobby sat around for a while in a mope and made remarks like this other guy, he must be a good lay, and other things that annoyed her. And then he popped some speed to "hurry things up." And it did. But when he was up—as he had been, it turns out, when they saw me from the rock—the dragon business all came back to him and it seemed real, she guessed, because he was pacing around talking a lot of crazy gibberish.

Bobby wasn't very literary, in fact not literary at all; however, he must have had a couple of semi-fundamentalist parents, because as Lilith described it, he began going on about a great throne and seven candlesticks, and seven stars, and a huge sword, and the keys of hell and death. And soon he was shouting about Balaam and Balac and how the Book was sealed with seven seals, and he snatched her alto recorder and displayed himself as four tootling angels at the four corners of the world. Then finally he dashed out of the house onto his motorcycle shouting he'd be back with the sword and then they'd see about the red dragon and all that God had made and would destroy.

Lilith, who was avant-garde enough that she'd never read the Bible, or hadn't read it to remember it, was puzzled by all these allusions. But there must be something immediate in the imagery that talks to people, because she got the general drift. She stewed around the house for a couple of hours, thinking she ought to come to me but remembering that Bobby had ominously predicted his return. So she waited, chomping celery again but unable to concentrate on Hesse.

When he came back he was in a spirit of great elation. He had somehow found a huge rusty broad sword and a gallon of red lacquer. And he was murmuring something about how there were foreheads to paint.

"God, I thought he was going to paint himself all up like an Indian, but he didn't. He became quite calm, and then he stood the sword in a corner with the paint can and brush, and he sat down and drank a beer and watched me.

But the look on his face was like very freaky; it really frightened me."

Then he started to talk quietly to her as if trying to explain something that was going to be very difficult for her to get through her beautiful dumb sweet head, but she couldn't make much out of it because it was all tied up in his mind with crazy animals like Leviathan and Behemoth and lambs and the water of life.

"I mean, y'know, I think he'd gone straight up like suddenly, so he was really preaching a whole lot of nonsense about Armageddon and what would I say to the Lord. I mean, is that stuff about the seven candles and all that in the Bible somewhere?"

"Yes, I believe it is."

"Gee, where did he get religion like? I mean he really surprised me with all that flaky stuff, and then he was trying to get me to repent. Said he'd even baptize me right then and there, holding the beer can over my head, if I'd say, 'Get thee behind me, Satan,' or something like that. Then I could lie down with the lamb, or, oh I dunno, I'm getting it all mixed up, because he was really MAD, stark insane."

I tried to explain by saying that when *he* thought about dragons he remembered them from the Bible, and dragons are given a very bad time in the Bible, which is why all those saints thought they had to tell stories about fighting them when they fought their sins and lust. That's what those dragons really were, and that's why we are so maligned. But I stopped because I was getting excited and it wasn't really relevant at the moment to start in on how the dragon was treated in human myth.

"Well, as long as he's high, he's thinking about you.

He's ready to come find you. He may even be on the way. I did all I could to put him off. I pleaded with him about it; I said he was all wrong, there wasn't any such thing, but I just couldn't like get through to him. Besides, he was drinking now too and pretty smashed, so I was just trying to get away."

"And you did."

"Finally, but it was awful because he sat there and told me how I'd sinned with the dragon and had to be saved, and had to acknowledge my sin, very coolly and explaining things like he was some mad psychiatrist or somebody with his head all full of therapy himself, you know—oh, I suppose you don't—the ones who are always trying to get you into a rap session, always trying to HELP you. Well, after all that, he got sorta frustrated because I wouldn't say anything. God, I was probably cowering for all I know. So he went to a tool chest and got this pair of work gloves. 'No blood on my hands,' he said, laughing sorta funny like, you know, like Frankenstein in the old comedies. And I really thought he was gonna strangle me, but I couldn't run for it. I had to wait for a chance. That's when he went and got the paint can and opened it and slopped the brush in it like a madman artist. So I took out for the door with him after me with the brush, shouting that he'd paint my forehead right now. But I got out and he tripped and fell over an old monkey wrench or something and I beat it outside and next door. Beat is right, I damned near beat the door down before the Flacks opened up, right in the middle of the ball game, and they didn't want to be bothered, y'know. But I was a sight with this bruised face and he really had me spooky and shaking. So we watched through the window, and he came outside like a big giant, carrying the paint can and brush, and he took the whole side of the house to write B-A-B-Y-L-O-N in great sloppy letters and they streamed like blood. Boy, the landlord will really freak out when he sees that. And then he shouted, 'Come out, Mother of Harlots,' and staggered back in.

"The Flacks wanted to call the police or the sheriff or someone, but I kept them from it. I pleaded with them that he was high and he'd come down soon and there'd be no harm to them, even though we heard a lot of noise and rummaging around next door. Pretty soon he came out again with the paintbrush and a quart of beer. He painted 'WHORE OF' above the 'BABYLON,' and then he took the beer bottle and broke it on the corner of the house, shouting 'Shove off,' got on his motorcycle, and wobbled off."

I reasoned that since he hadn't taken his sword, he'd not started out to slay me yet. He'd go back for it.

"But I think we can expect him up here. I mean, he has this crazy idea that you're the whore's steed. And he'll bring some help with him, I bet."

Every Beowulf needs his Wiglaf. The truth was that through all of history there had been very few attacks on dragons by individuals, except now and then when a crazy monk would throw himself into a dragon-fight in order to achieve a place in the Lives of the Saints. I supposed Bobby would round up a few of his rider friends, and so did Lilith, who didn't think they'd be much help in a crisis.

She was very upset. "Oh, Firedrake, I'm so sorry. I'm guilty of bringing all this on. There's something about me, I guess. I always get into the middle of a disaster." At the moment I didn't want to cater to her self-dramatization or to hear a catalogue of things she'd been in the middle of. I was only hoping I could get her to go away for a little while or take a long sleep. Bobby would not come until morning, and I needed the time to move at least the Greater Chalice to safety.

I didn't hint around, though, because I suspected that she was in no mood to take a hint. She was nervous and pacing the Outer Hall in circles, touching everything, patting objects without really thinking about what they were. I suggested we have some mead. Normally I drink in solitude, and not much at any one time. Now, it seemed to me that she required something to relax her. I broke my habit.

There is nothing like mead. I poured out two small liqueur glasses of the stuff, brewed by myself after Dad's formula. We sat facing each other, she sipping from the glass. This drinking with a human being presents a trivial problem for us. We have two choices, to pour the contents of the glass into our gullets, with our heads thrown back and jaws gaping, or to lap. The lapping is difficult in a small mead glass because of our large forked tongue. Nevertheless, I chose to lap—in a way; that is, I allowed one of the forks to dip itself daintily into the glass. Actually this isn't a bad procedure with mead, for it provides one with a complete and drawn-out taste of the stuff, particularly if one has already determined which fork is most sensitive to mead's taste. I had done that.

Watching me managing the glass and my tongue actually did more to relax her than the mead. She was highly amused. I'll admit I was somewhat embarrassed, and finally I said, "Well, you can see that dragons have a few problems and awkwardnesses, too."

"Yes, it makes me feel better somehow. I mean the way

you've managed to deal with it so gracefully. It took a lot of practice, not knocking over the glass and all that, didn't it? It's almost an inspiration. If you don't at first succeed . . ." For a moment I thought my ear was being pulled, but she wasn't ironic. When she had finished up her mead, she fell back relaxed on the pile of pillows in the corner. "Y'know," she said, "I'd just sorta like to stay here."

"That's all right. You can stay here tonight. No need to go back." I knew it would be better for me if she did go back, but I had a feeling that she really had no safe place to go and I'd better take the chance with her here rather than have her wandering around Southern California or getting it in her mind to go back to mad saintly Bobby, which I suspected she probably would do.

"But that's not what I mean. I mean like all the time. Not just tonight. Why couldn't I just live with you? Like a pet or something."

I bristled my triangles. "Who's a pet?" I growled.

She laughed. "Oh, *pardon* me. I didn't mean to insult you. I meant I'd be the pet. I mean I've been a pet before. C'mon now, Firedrake, all those stories about you guys and chicks can't be total lies, can they? After all, you have wrapped me up in your tail."

I averted my eyes from her. She was wriggling around getting comfortable or something on those pillows. I placed my tongue in the mead, then gathered my suavity together and contemplated her coolly. I began to wonder a bit whether indeed all those stories were total lies. If they weren't they must have come about rather in this way, I thought, with a lot of help from the young lady. But no! Not a dragon under *Geis*.

"I mean, I'm strong and healthy, and I could become a

vegetarian or we could steal enough food for me, and
there's really no reason for me to go back, is there? Anyway we could try it. I'd really like to, Firedrake."

If only they possessed some sort of *Wyrd* of their own,
I thought. Why, then it might really work out, human
beings and dragons. But I shook my head sadly, and she
turned serious. "Well," she said, "I haven't been rejected
too many times before."

I believed that.

March 31

I am telling all this shortly after the sun has arisen.
Last night after I listened Lilith to sleep and spoke into
the recorder, I went to work. The choice was whether to
take the Chalice or the chest of balm. I chose the Chalice because of its greater value, even though I know that
in leaving the chest I have put temptation in Lilith's way.
It was a choice that had to transcend my knowledge of her
presence. Who would tolerate a vision of the Chalice being
passed from hand to hand among those who come with
Bobby up into these hills?

The job accomplished, I returned at dawn to find Lilith still asleep. There was time to look once again at the
domain I would be quitting. I had come to accept that my
procrastination had made it unlikely, no, impossible for me
to rescue the most prized objects in my collections.

So I descended to commune with the Marmon and Ultimate Model T. There they stood in the subdued light
that I had designed for them. It was as if my freeing them

from their highways and my re-creation of them had charged them with something greater than life, the peace and strength of their own forms, these Michigan shapes that teased me into admiration. In their simple presence even the dedicated life of a dragon seemed but a dreary linear series of happenings. As I had worked upon them the idea of their completed forms had engendered in me an aesthetic appreciation. Now they accomplished more than that. They were all sublime, like primitive gods. From Earth's greatest store their elements had come. When I closed these halls, they would sink back into the primal matter, rusting away slowly over the ages, rejoining Earth, returning to the central core. There was nothing of plastic in them. It is clear why one must hate styrofoam.

Leaving the alcove, I stopped for a moment before my collection of bottles. There my feelings were less profound. Images of containment and protection—as compared with the autos, which suggested quest and movement—my bottles always conjured for me the past, a more quiet, innocent age. They lacked magnitude. But this was not the proper time for remembrance. In a few hours, perhaps minutes, only the present would be crucial, the past past, the future in the balance.

I had been in the depths long enough. I was impatient for what the day would bring.

It was all depressingly clear. Someone once said that if you managed to erase a whole generation of human beings the next one would come along and fill all the old slots. Which is to say that there's probably been nothing really new for centuries in dragon-fighting. We are still the same, still bound by our *Wyrd;* and human beings keep inheriting the dragon-fighters' roles. Oh, the horse is steel now, and there are flame throwers almost equal to our natural talents. But the state of mind, that's the same. I could see Bobby this very moment in huge activity, gathering his forces. When Cervantes wrote about Quixote he gave him a companion, Sancho, and thereby edged up a bit on the truth, Cervantes being a realist after all. The point is that, tormented into dragon-hate, they always have to go around converting other people to the fight. They have to call for action and not words, and they have to demand total fealty, and they have to whip up reasons why the old dragon in the hills simply has to go. He is evil, or the Roman Church, or monopoly capital—almost anything will serve. The saint will exercise his revenge against life by implicating everyone else, and a lot of people won't ask any questions, because of the fundamental barbarism in all of them, I suppose. Here I'm condensing Knäckerune's famous song. I, pythonosopher.

So in my mind's eye I had no trouble locating Bobby heading out on his motorcycle to collect the gang, still high on dragon vision, drugged by belief, but believing with all the old allegorical trappings, never grasping the meaning of real dragons, never acknowledging our otherness from his guilt. First his followers would think him insane and laugh and josh at him, and he would be furious, but he is possessed of the TRUTH now, so he persists. Some of them will come along because they are humoring Old Bob and what the hell. Others will come along because they don't have anything else to do this day, and then there'll be a few, a very few, maybe only twelve or so, who will come along because if they don't believe there is a dragon in the hills they could be convinced by seeing one. In short, they don't disbelieve. Bob was very eloquent when he called upon them, and they almost thought, even wanted to think, there was something to it. How simple to put all one's evil into a dragon and slay it! Maybe one or two of these people came along because if there was anything to it there was something in it for them. So I could see them congregating and circling in the street and varooming their engines and laughing and joking and bugging each other with tall outlandish insults. And Bobby would get up on the porch of some old house with wild vision in his eyes and the eloquence of his certainty, shouting at them that if they didn't want to fight a real goddamned dragon, if they didn't want to go out and punish sin, they'd better not follow along, and that he came here with a sword, which he swung in the air. A few of them would laugh at the sin bit and put it up to Bobby's being high, this sin thing could be taken too far, but they'd follow along because every once in a while maybe some talk about sin was a good thing, and, anyway, who knows?

So, swinging his sword above his head, he'd leap to horse and lead the whole noisy exhaust-fuming pack down the road out to the highway, onward rolling as to war.

Having watched it all in my mind's eye, I stepped outside into the cool, dewy dawn and took in the high air, still soft and damp from the sea. I shall miss it in my new surroundings. I had it in my mind to visit the owl, for I knew that before I moved, and before Bobby came, I wished to discover whether owls had *Wyrds* and, if so, whether the owl was ambivalent about his or not—that is, in respect to its relation to human beings. I was feeling quite exhausted by Lilith and Bobby, certainly, and yet I was not really questioning my own *Wyrd*, merely whether the owl thought he played a significant role in human life.

The owl was perched in the usual Oak. I began by making a number of vague remarks about the strangeness of human beings and their desires. The owl perched, watching me. Then I made a mistake. I asked, forgetting that he might fly off, "Do you think that human beings understand your role, that is, is their symbolization of you your reality?" The owl became very agitated. His head swiveled, he looked in all directions, he hopped along the branch. Finally he hooted and flew away. It was a depressing moment to know there were others like us, and without voice. It was unfortunate also not to find out about his *Wyrd,* if he had one. I had been seeking for some communion in a world suddenly *other.*

Depressed, I strolled on in the direction of the tarn. In a small meadow the daffodils had bloomed and seemed to be calling to be taken. I picked about a dozen of them for a bouquet. I have just put them in a vase near Lilith, who is still sleeping. Her cheekbone is bruised. She seems at peace, yet she is not. Her id, her censor, her superego, and the rest are at work as ever in the caverns, the Outer and Great Halls, of her humanity.

April 2

I wish now to report on the tumultuous events of two days ago. Some minutes before they arrived one could hear the droning noise of the motorcycles as they wound into the hills. Lilith had slept soundly all night and into the morning. When she awoke to the tap of my claw she murmured, "Daffodils, that's nice," and wanted to roll over, face to the wall again. But I kept tapping her awake and told her Bobby was on the way, she must stay there and not come out of the barrow and, above all, not descend into the Great Hall. It was futile to mention this; I even considered saying nothing out of fear that I'd merely renew her curiosity. I could not stay long enough to frighten her (she was too sleepy anyway) or impress her again with the seriousness of my warning. The motorcycles would be taking the turns and twists now on the last hill before mine, and I would have to be ready, watching.

When they came, they came in high good spirits, whooping and yelling down from the road, and I observed them as I crouched inside the barrow entrance behind the vines and shrubs that blocked the low flat entrance. It was still possible that they would not find the entrance, but I was not counting on it. I would hide as long as I could, and if found I would try to frighten them away. But I was not certain that my fright plan would repel them. If it did not I would have to shed their blood, which is something that a dragon does not like to do.

And so they came running into the field from the road, and I realized there was one aspect of this thing I had not anticipated. It was the women. For every one of the dozen or so men there apparently was a woman, laughing and cavorting through the tall grass, some scrambling up onto the rock where I had first seen Bobby and Lilith, some running down to the edge of the tarn. In all manner of dress they were, from black jeans and jackets to print bikinis to hiphugger slacks and halters to what in some cases was soon nothing as they stripped and frolicked about in my tarn, swimming, blowing spouts of water, splashing at the men on the shore, until some of the men hustled off their clothes, too, and dove in. Then the laughing became screaming and shrieking.

I was interested enough that I nearly missed Bobby's appearance. He came walking from his motorcycle to the road edge and surveyed the scene like some Roman general. If I had not expected him he would have been unrecognizable. His beard seemed longer. His hair flowed down well below his collar, and it appeared to be combed, parted in the middle. The black jacket and black jeans were not in evidence. There was no Nazi cap. He wore a white shirt open at the front and white jeans now. He was Mr. Clean and Jesus all rolled into one. And he held a big broad sword. I wondered where in the world he had found it. Why, I didn't have anything remotely up to it in my collection. Normally, I would have coveted it right then and there, but there wasn't really time, I guess. I didn't even think of it that way.

While the women frolicked in the tarn, swimming about, raising their buttocks in the air and diving underwater, jumping up and down in the shallow places, and calling the men to follow them, Bobby stood watching, silent and angry on the road edge. The others seemed to have come for a picnic or for the hell of it; at the moment they were completely out of his control, which goes to suggest that people never did go on so-called dragon hunts to hunt dragons but simply to enjoy nature, have a picnic, swim, and lie around in the sun like lizards. Bobby was having the trouble that all those human beings who are suddenly possessed of a quest must suffer. There are few natural questers among the troops. He could not talk to them or even shout at them effectively because of the noise they made and the fun they were having; for indeed these human beings seemed to gambol in the water with the spirit of dragons themselves. They were loving it, and even each other—right there in the water. When that sort of thing gets underway there is very little that any St. George can do.

So Bobby stood there grimly, in a sort of disgust, watching the deterioration of the fighting morale of his troops, so to speak. Two lieutenants flanking him gesticulated to each other and laughed nervously, sometimes applauding the rather interesting acrobatic efforts of their friends in the tarn, but obviously restraining themselves in sight of their stern general. Suddenly, though, one of them peeled off his shirt and began to run toward the tarn, shouting, "Hey, Sally, hey Sally, hey watch that, hey, hey, like wait for me." At the edge of the shore he leapt out of his pants and hit the water with a flat racer's dive in the direction of a spaniel-wet blonde who had just swum naked into the arms of some accommodating motorcyclist.

Bobby was furious. He danced a sort of jig in his anger and then pitched his sword into the ground. It quivered there. He stared at it a moment, then stamped the dirt around it. He looked glumly at the tarn, turned to his last remaining aide, pulled the sword out of the ground again, gestured at the aide and shouted at the frolickers (two had run from the water and were making love on the rock; another, who had sprinted up the hill, was returning now with a six-pack of beer; still others ran through the tall grass and daffodils). Someone was picking the daffodils and throwing them in the air, picking them up again and throwing them in the air. Someone had a transistor, and there was music. Three blondes stood in a triangle, clapping in various rhythms. Dancing began. The girls clapped on. They were transporting themselves.

If it hadn't been for Bobby it would have been a heart-warming scene indeed. It was news for the Delphic oracle, actually. Under other conditions I would have elected to join in, rising at some dramatic moment from the underground stream to rustle the waters and frolic with them, perhaps to flick my tail about and scatter them like minnows with a good crazy story to tell back in town.

But Bobby had written them off for the present. He was waving his sword and scything the grass as he walked. He was obviously bent on learning where the barrow entrance was and he'd walk the whole terrain to find it. He was possessed of the quest. The one remaining lieutenant wandered aimlessly behind him, picking a wildflower here and there, turning to watch the play in the tarn when there was a special shriek or general laughter. Bobby would turn to him now and then and mutter or gesticulate an order. For a moment the lieutenant would be a show of alert questing activity, but as soon as Bobby turned away all of the tension would drain from the follower's body, and both eyes and body would wander. There just isn't enough dedication to dragon-fighting in human beings to make them a constant threat to us.

Suddenly Bobby stopped and stared at the ground before him. He turned, excited, and beckoned to his follower. They were both quickly on their knees looking at something in the clay. They were about thirty yards directly before me. I realized with annoyance what it was. That morning, preoccupied with the owl's anxiety, I had neglected to take care about clawprints. In the damp dewy clay of the terrain I had left my mark. Lieutenant, prodded into action by the real, flew like a bat to the tarn, waving his arms and shouting, while Bobby crouched over my clawprint watching, watching furtively, at the ready.

A few returned, leaping and shouting and gamboling as they came, until they, too, were crouching, in the altogether, as we say, peering down at the print. Then there was much arguing and joshing, because it didn't look like any goddamned footprint to some of them, and to others it did. To enough of them, because soon all of the troop were surrounding the footprint, and Bobby was shouting instructions that some of them may have been willing to follow. It appeared that a modicum of order was about to prevail. A few raced back to the motorcycles. Some of the girls carried picnic supplies down from the road, the first topless waitresses I had more than read about. Pans and spoons were produced and distributed, and soon there was a fearful noise. About ten of them raced about in the tall grass beating the pans with spoons or sticks and shouting, "Come out, come out, we know you're there," and laughing as they ran. They were amiable enough. The din would have routed out a sturdy lion, though.

Bobby was visibly angry at them. They were offending him and the whole idea of his quest, these silly thoughtless naked girls and motorcyclists. They were as frivolous as the Blue Nicors. The whole dragon hunt had taken on the air of a carnival or a rite of spring. The girls were running in a circle now, beating their pans, and then it was a chase. Round and round among the Oaks they ran, with the men in pursuit, and one by one they fell exhausted in the tall grass and were seen no more for a while. The beating of the pans subsided, and Bobby, his lieutenant, and another who had joined him stood alone, staring down at the footprint.

Then Bobby looked up suddenly, directly at the bushes guarding the slit of my barrow. He stared a long time. I was staring back, well camouflaged within the shadows. The two lieutenants were distracted. With jovial appreciation they observed a bare human behind wavering at tall-grass level. Alone, sword in hand, Bobby came tentatively toward me, beckoning to his cohorts. They turned reluctantly from the action and followed haltingly, then, intrigued by his tense, careful manner, fell several paces to the rear. They were humoring him, but on the other hand they weren't entirely sure——

I had to make my move, and so I parted the brush with my snout and protruded it. Struck dumb he was. The other two turned tail and ran for the rock, through the assorted lovers in the grass. Bobby tensed there, grasping his huge sword, waiting for the worst. In truth he hadn't the slightest idea how to fight a dragon.

The naked people in the grass stood up one by one now, and the men retreated slowly toward the road. With dispatch, however, the women picked up their pans and sticks. Spreading across the terrain as if by plan, they advanced on me behind Bobby. I emerged slowly and menacingly, growling and snorting flame high in the air. One of the women emitted a long piercing scream. Communal low howling ensued, and then they were beating their infernal pans and running in a huge circle around me.

There had been nothing like this in the west since General Custer, I thought to myself. It was the last levity of the day. I had to put up a huge wall of fire as I advanced, swinging my flame to the right and left like a wild firehose. As I did so I drove the circle of women farther back. They hurled the most abominable language at me and cursed me as if I were some awful devil upon whose blood they were intent. Bobby tried to stand his ground for a moment, but the heat of my short blasts, designed to force him away, was, of course, successful. Saints are willing to risk burning by other human beings or by themselves, but not by dragons. I singed the two lieutenants, setting their voluminous hair aflame, and they ran screaming to the tarn. I could hear motorcycles being gunned on the road. Bobby retreated to the rock now, where he tried to rally his depleted forces, waving his sword and berating the cowards about him. I broke the circle of prancing women. Spraying flame in an arc of a hundred and eighty degrees, I drove those who persisted before me in rout toward the tarn. Past Bobby I went, driving my herd.

One tall blonde I must not have noticed. Apparently she had hidden behind an Oak and, as I passed, she leaped out and with tremendous agility landed on my back. Straddling me, wedged between two triangles, she clawed for a handhold in my leathery back, reached finally to grasp an ear with each hand. I shook like a dog, but she would not let go. I waved my tail to give my shaking more momentum, but she was tenacious. I did not want to roll over upon her for fear of hurting her badly. It was clear that I had a berserk on my back. I had heard that there were genuine female berserks in the days of Cerridwen worship, but never had I seen one. There was nothing to do but head for the tarn and force her off into the water. With the others running before me, I loped to the shore, shook again mightily, tried everything I could think of to buck her off into the water. I could hear Bobby shouting from the rock in the midst of the screaming of those swimming about: "Whore, bitch, abomination, drunk with the blood." I looked back to check on him. As I suspected, he had thought this his opportunity, for suddenly he made a great leap from the rock, tripped, fell, struggled to his feet, found his sword, and advanced upon me as I writhed and shook to free myself of the girl. It was no good. I would have to dive into the tarn and hope that she would give up her hold in the water; I did so, as the others scattered like polliwogs for the shore. Down deep I went. She stayed with me for a short time, but then I felt my ears released, and I looked up through the murk to see her rising to the surface with accomplished strokes. I could not resist surfacing in the center of the tarn and ruffling the waters mightily. I observed Bobby knee-deep on the shore, beating my waves with his weapon. He was in a rage, indeed. And he was abandoned. The others had had enough, even my tall blonde equestrienne, who was limping slowly up the hill to a more trustworthy steed.

From the center of the tarn I stared at Bobby, and he looked daggers at me. "Bring back Lilith, you . . . you . . ." What could he call me? "You, you goddamned dragon, you—Leviathan!" I fired one last ball across his brow and set his hair aflame. He ducked into the water, shook, turned and ran up the hill, shouting and gesticulating at me. I dived again, this time toward the underground stream entrance, hoping and indeed thinking that he would not dare to enter the barrow now. But I had second thoughts and returned to the surface to make sure. I could see him running about near the rock, collecting items of clothing in a kind of frenzy. He was no longer carrying his sword. I watched some minutes of this frantic activity, and then he disappeared over the road's crest. Shortly the machine varoomed.

I was much relieved. I swam not directly to the stream but once about the tarn swiftly as a seal, breaking the water with my back and sending ripples, then actual waves, in all directions toward the shore. In truth, I felt that I had not come off badly. Yes, they would tell tall stories of dragon-fighting, and no doubt there would be expeditions to this area, but by morning I would be far away, the Hoard under effective protection. I would be far more careful in the future. I swam faster and with great glee until the waves rushed at the shore and there was noise of them in the trees and the hills. I rejoiced because I needed only the next several hours of this day and the night to transport the last chest.

The last chest! Where was Lilith now? This time I dived deep, adjusted my frontal lamp, and found the dark stream's entrance. I hurried through its windings, swift as a Nicor, and emerged where the stream flows into the Great Hall immediately opposite alcove six—the alcove of the chest of balm. Shaking off the water as I emerged, I knew at once I might be too late, for the Great Hall was illuminated and, beyond Lilith, framed in the entrance, I could see the chest standing open. It struck me forcefully at this moment in the fine illumination my electricianship had provided that it was now doubly mad for her to seek the urn. In that light, standing there transfixed for a moment by desire, she possessed all of the beauty necessary to her life. She deserved to have her portrait painted. She was all she needed to be. She held the precious urn before her, and slowly she began to lift off its golden cap. The gold and the dragon-embossed urn itself were nothing to her; only its contents would satisfy her now. I shouted sternly, and she turned, startled.

"What are you doing here? I told you to stay away from the chest. You must put down the urn. Put it down." I crept toward her. "Put it down," I repeated. I did not want to hurt her but could not protect her by destroying the urn with my fires. She stared at me blankly, robotlike. It was as if she were dazed. We both stood frozen, then slowly she closed the chest and placed the urn upon it. I crept forward again, but she reached for the urn as if to warn me. She was somehow not Lilith. Proximity to the treasure had rendered her an object with a single will. She could resist the treasure now only by a huge countereffort and my help. But the object she had become was wary of me. It would threaten me if it could.

I could get no closer. I pleaded with her to leave the alcove. I insisted that she must come away from the treasure within minutes or be changed unutterably by it. If she took the treasure, even touched the urn's contents, she would be destroyed. I watched the real Lilith struggle with her desire. She turned to the urn, then to me; tears came to her clouded, thoughtless eyes. I argued and pleaded and threatened, never mentioning the matter of beauty, never revealing the exact result of the balm's use, and for a moment I believed that I had won. She stepped toward me dully, the back of her hand across her brow, as if she were very tired, near collapse. I know she was ready to come all the way except at that moment there was a stirring in the tunnel and Bobby, muddy-white in his saintly jeans, burst into our presence. His sword abandoned, he stood there, his beard burnt to stubble and his hair singed short. He held a small rifle or carbine at hip height. Poor Bobby, he had sprung into the room in a parody of some western gunman or commando. He had earned Lilith's scorn. He looked at Lilith, who mocked him with her eyes, and then at me, unable to decide upon whom to level his sights. Neither she nor I spoke. I was profoundly disgusted with myself. I had allowed Bobby to play the oldest trick in the world upon me. I had thought him so defeated, so frustrated, that he would not return alone. I had underestimated his saintly fanaticism.

He chose me first, as if to duel me with his carbine. On four legs I presented no really vulnerable target to him, for we are impervious to rifle fire in every region of our body except the eyes and certain hidden areas of the belly. But, of course, he did not know this, nor did Lilith. Before he could fire at me, and before I had the presence of mind to place myself between him and Lilith, she had somehow turned back into herself. She stood glaring haughtily at Bobby. She had purposely attracted his attention away from me. And then, laughing, she shouted at him, "You're ridiculous, Bobby. Look at you. You're ridiculous. You're just so, just so goddamned *human.*" And she turned back to the chest, picked up the urn.

We were both transfixed, Bobby and I, for a moment. In dumb show, she appeared unreal as she calmly opened the urn, dipped a forefinger into it, and turned toward us. I know now that at this very moment Earth trembled, the lights swayed on their chandeliers, and strange shadows played all about us. It had not seemed important then. Bobby shouted a warning at her, screaming not to touch the stuff, to come out of there, to . . . but he ended sobbing and shouting, "Whore, bitch, Babylon." As her finger went to her cheek he fired the carbine direct upon her. It was too late to touch the real Lilith, for when the bullet reached her breast it merely shattered the cold marble statue that she had become. In one fraction of a second I saw her, and perhaps Bobby saw her, in her cold and inhuman marble form, an image of perfect beauty. No doubt the scar over her eye had been expunged by this greatest of all sculptors and the nose had been straightened a bit. No doubt the sculptor had improved her figure here and there and given to her eyes whatever perfection was beyond them as they had been. No human Pygmalion could have accomplished such a statue, and no Pygmalion could have loved it, only stood in mute admiration of its inhuman otherness.

Bobby stood helplessly above the shattered marble, then sank to his knees before it. He held the carbine limply. He was sobbing. He turned to look at me. I had not moved a muscle of tail or leg. His face showed nothing but contorted pain and welling rage. Watching me, he crawled toward the urn, which lay on its side where Lilith had dropped it at the moment of her metamorphosis.

Watching me every moment, he felt for the urn. He would take it from me and destroy it, he said. It was evil, and so was I, and I had brought about her death, and there would be no more of it!

I watched his hand all the way to the urn, and then finally I incinerated him. On the floor lay the carbine. When the flame subsided in a few seconds, for it was a brilliantly hot fireball I belched at him, nothing but ash remained. As it happened, Earth in His outrage shook slightly again. The tremor was longer, though not as sharp as the first. I looked to the ceiling. Dust and soot were falling from it. In the alcove a huge crack appeared across the face of Gwynfyd's portrait. The ceiling began to sag. I leaped to save the urn. Deftly I found the gold cover, secured it to the urn, and, grasping it in one claw, loped quickly across the Great Hall. As I made for the tunnel, I looped my tail tip through the handle of the box that houses this tape recorder.

Into the tunnel I darted. Behind me Earth was rumbling, over my shoulder I saw the ceiling of the alcove give way and the wall of Gwynfyd's portrait collapse upon the chest and the shattered marble statue. A brief cloud of fine ashes hung over the entrance. The lights dimmed and were extinguished.

I rushed on ahead to the Outer Hall, where I stopped for only a second near Lilith's couch, snatching up impetuously in my six foreteeth a few stalks of the daffodil bouquet. From the tunnel came a clapping noise and a rush of dust. The Great Hall had no doubt collapsed. I moved quickly to the barrow entrance. Lilith and Bobby were buried by Earth.

My mind now raced over the last few moments and my own errors of strategy beginning with the occasion on which I had allowed Lilith into the barrow itself. Yet it was Bobby upon whom my mind most dwelt—Bobby and his divine madness. Like all those crazy monomaniacal saints before him, he had found it necessary to cast his dragon in the role of evil. Was this a necessary human act? When the others returned to town or wherever they went, would they complete Bobby's story for him? Would his disappearance take on the aura of human myth? Would they provide him with a transfiguration that his life could not achieve? Would some ragged band of singers and flute-players on street corner or campus sing new songs about a dragon-slayer? He would become in myth his own mad ideal of himself, while Lilith's real apotheosis remained the dragon's secret. Perhaps all would be well again for a time, the price great, but the Hoard saved.

I emerged from the barrow with the urn in one claw, the daffodils in my jaw, and the tape recorder hung on my tail. I thought nothing of it at the time but I was a strange sight, surely. I looked about cautiously, very cautiously, for I had enjoyed quite enough human company for this day. All was quiet in Sun's afternoon except for a slight breeze rustling the Oaks. I did not speak to them. They would disapprove of my having picked the flowers, and it would take too long to explain that I had done in Bobby and thereby get back in their good graces. They hated humankind. I turned to make my way toward the rock.

It was a great shock seeing them there, two naked bodies, sunning. They were left over from the dragon hunt or returned from it, perhaps. They were both blonde and long-haired, of sex different, and they lay very quietly loving Sun. I glanced at the road above. Two motorcycles stood propped there, and I imagined Lilith's Volkswagen farther back. I tried to creep by very quietly, but the girl (I am beginning to think the female of the species has acute dragon sense) sat up suddenly and stared at me.

"Hey, the dragon's back," she said, shaking her friend's shoulder.

"Mmh."

"Hey, like he's back and he has these daffodils in his mouth."

"Yeah."

Apprehended, I could no longer sneak by. Instead I approached to a discreet distance, waved my head and tossed the daffodils in the direction of that pretty, all tan, all blonde, orange-blossomy sweetheart.

"Gee," she said. "Gee, thanks, sir, I mean, Mr. Dragon.

Thanks." She hopped down from the rock to pick up the stalks. She was a lovely thing, indeed.

Kneeling, she said, "Joe here, he's asleep and sorta out of it, or he'd thank you, too."

I left it at that, with a royal bow to the charming young lady. She knelt there, cradling the flowers as if they were a huge Miss America bouquet or something, and watched me gravely. I passed by, treading as softly as a dragon may, past the rock, toward the crest of my hill to the broad plateau above. I would travel by day now, and not through the tunnels, since the quake. A few yards past the rock, I turned and looked back. She was watching me. She did not want me to go. She was much impressed with me, I could tell. I said to myself as I turned east up the hill, what use did I have for a few old bedraggled daffodils, what use indeed? Why, I kept saying, I could hardly remember now what caused me to pick them. But dragons always remember, and the game I played with myself was merely a game.

"So long, dragon baby," she called to me as I came to the road. There was another short Earth tremor, and I heard her trying to wake up Joe on the rock. And so the last battle in the west ended.

My attention shifted now to what lay before me, the trip to my new halls and the care with which I must cherish the urn in my claw. I looked up and down the road, and then I saw below me, coming up the incline, the three real-estate men again, followed this time by three stragglers in flowered sports shirts, shorts, and string ties with medallions. They were pushing ever onward toward the crest where I now stood. When the leading three saw me, their faces broke into the smiles familiar from my last encounter, and their hands shot forth in unison to prepare for shaking my claw. Behind them the three stragglers waved and smiled and took out their cameras. They were all still twenty or thirty yards away, hands thrust forward, broad styrofoam smiles on their round, well-shaved faces, when it happened.

Earth really shook this time. Then there was a huge searing crack, and quite suddenly the ground fell away at my feet. I jumped back, startled, as the fissure widened. Slowly and majestically, like the wall of a building collapsing, all of Earth to the west fell away. It was as if the whole of the globe were breaking in two. The three real-estate men and their clients kept walking, arms extended in greeting, smiles never fading, up the tottering incline, and slowly with Earth they fell away, still walking. Very slowly they fell away. Finally there came a crashing, tumultuous roar, and the fading cliff of raw ground that I faced crumbled before me. Slowly, from miles away in the west, the sea began to trickle in far below. Trickling, then running in streams, then in huge avalanches and boiling into whirlpools it came, filling new-made valleys and overflowing the piled up peaks of ground, until after a time only a few small islands remained in the whirling foam. And at last they, too, disappeared.

I stood high on the cliff observing the boiling sea below. As far to the north and to the south as I could see, Earth had rent away its Pacific shore, and all was water. I haunched there staring at the sea for a long time. Huge tidal waves ripped at the new coastland, and some of it gave way to the sea. My rocky promontory remained steadfast. I did not wish yet to move. Something kept me at the spot, something was telling me to wait. As afternoon wore on, I recognized that the sky had changed. Sun was preparing to set over the ocean, and He was neither as large nor as red as I had become accustomed to seeing Him. I realized that there was no smog along this coast now, only the mist settling from the turmoil of the sea.

After a while, with Sun just above the horizon, the sea calmed somewhat and began to resume its usual pattern of swells and breakers upon the new shoreline. Soon, I surmised, there would roll in upon the beach a variety of floating objects. I did not relish the opportunity to observe what the sea would kick up to land from its new depths.

Then out to the southwest I noticed a strange commotion in the water. There were seabirds hovering and screaming, a welcome sound to me, who had lived so long inland. Gradually the commotion moved toward me in the waves, and the birds hung about it in the air. I could not make out what it was.

Yards offshore, the waters parted and a great head appeared, like a huge seal looking about. It was one of my own. I was so amazed by this appearance that I nearly dropped the urn of balm upon the cliff's rocks. The dragon came ashore directly below me, looked up to where I stood, and waved.

He was a beautiful creature, of years about four hundred, I would say, deeply encrusted with amethysts, with much blue and streaks of gold. He shook the water of his journey from his back, and shouted up at me, "Hey, Dad, I hope you have a good tarn where I can loosen these barnacles."

I was speechless as I haunched there watching. He was finding his way up the cliffside with great agility and speed. I could hear him singing as he came, "Hate California, it's cold and it's damp."

At the top of the cliff, I saw him shoot a fireball of modest proportions over the side, raise himself up on his hind legs, and come to embrace me. "I bet you thought I'd never come. Better late than never, and not a bit too soon, it seems. Hey, I see you've got the urn. That was some spectacle you arranged for me. Hasn't been anything like that in eons. Los Angeles is gone, I mean out of sight."

For the moment I had nothing to say.

April 3

Three days have passed since the last battle in the west that is no more. Cythrawl has spent much time soaking in the tarn, crusted as he was with salt and barnacles after his long journey. All is quiet here, but people have tramped to the coast in large groups despite warnings of another possible tremor. Last night I spoke to Feuerkugel of the quake, and he reported that San Francisco is no more. While Cythrawl has been soaking and resting, I have sat at my new barrow entrance in the shade of an outcropping of rock. My mind considers dragon life, while Cythrawl talks on about the virtues of tarn water. Clearly Gwynfyd schooled him well in pythonosophy.

There is less to be said for me. I have tried to tell him the story of my centuries here and how the events of three days ago impelled Earth to cast up the sea upon the west and how I am in part responsible for Earth's decision. I have told him that man will come again to this new coast and build tracts and resorts, then towns and cities, and these new halls will have to be vacated for higher, drier, more remote land, east even of Bakersfield. It will be difficult work, exploring the new terrain, choosing the site, hollowing the new tunnels, and moving the chests and chalices in the night.

April 4

It is now 4:00 A.M. Sun will soon be rising. Cythrawl and I have toured the tunnels. I have shown him where there is still work of shoring up to be done. I have spoken to him of the earthmovers. I have warned him against chance travelers in the hills. I think it unnecessary to have done so. The story of my time here has made him most thoughtful. There is one newly discovered dragon compulsion, or perhaps temptation, that I have mentioned to him, since little is said of it, except in passing, in the *Great Blerwm*. It is the temptation that comes upon us occasionally in life when suddenly we wish to be believed in. It is a dangerous temptation, unless our *Wyrd* be changed, because it leads to the desire to be acknowledged important and beautiful. Unfortunately, our importance cannot be fully appreciated by man without his grasping the real value and the ideal reality of the Hoard. And so . . . Few will believe in us, even come to see us as we are; and we are a grave danger to those who do.

The whole story of this matter I have now told, but I doubt that there will be believers in my tale, fewer certainly than compose the cult of Bobby and his dragon myth. I now understand that my work speaks really to dragons, though it began as an expression of the very desire I now warn against. It cannot be incorporated into the

Blerwm without aesthetic disorder. It is not alliterative, and it is in prose. Perhaps other dragons know the meaning of the story anyway, and only I have had to learn it. On the other hand, maybe the human poet I met at the dump was right. Perhaps, to shore up against the ruin of the world, dragons must reconsider the ways of centuries and begin revealing themselves to men, with all the dangers that implies. Is it after all an act of faith—blind, perhaps—that impels me not to destroy these tapes?

It is late now. Cythrawl and I have embraced, and I have set out across the terrain toward the seacliffs. I shall leave this recorder somewhere on the coast and slip into the sea. Shall I see Corrib again, or shall I meet the White Nicors in the Atlantic deep?

A Note on the Text

by Sigurd Drachesdrockh
Professor of Literotherapy
and Germanic Philology,
Hughes University

In the Ogden Lindwurmer Collection of the Hughes Library there has resided for many years a group of manuscript diaries that can be classified as belonging to Western Americana. Among these was found, about five years ago, an iron box marked with curious mandala-like symbols. It contained an old tape recorder. The tape tells the story presented here as *The Truth About Dragons: An Anti-Romance.* How the recorder came into the Lindwurmer Collection, or into the Hughes Library, for that matter, is not at all clear. It may have resided in the Rare Book Room for some years. A former curatress, now deceased, is known to have protected the materials under her care with almost dragonlike devotion. The tape cannot be older than 1972, and it may well be that the whole story and the placing of the box in the collection is the result of a hoax of much later date. Some external evidence points to the machinations of a former faculty member at Hughes, Paul M. Wormheidt, who is known to have placed other spurious maps and diary entries in the archives.

Before beginning to speculate on the internal evidence, one may profit from reviewing the meager external facts. In the years after the great quake of March 31, 1972, people in huge numbers traversed the new shoreline of the California coast, collecting, as sightseers will do, relics of that tragic occurrence. Directly inland from what had been the town of Nixon, California, formerly San Clemente (renamed in early 1972 for the President who vacationed there), there came hordes of elderly sightseers from the desert retirement communities. At all times of the day one could see them standing solemnly, facing the ocean. It was said that the President, Vice-President, and the Cabinet had not been drowned or swept away under the earth by the quake, that they would return one day from the west. But that was a sentimental story, indeed some thought it a Communist plot to weaken the fiber of our civil life. In fact, it was a myth, with as little truth to it as the reports that large fire-breathing creatures had been seen everywhere in Santa Barbara days before the quake occurred, and that a sea monster had surfaced off Santa Catalina Island on the thirtieth. The author of the tape was clearly aware of these stories, both of which were reported in the Las Vegas newspapers shortly after quake day. Indeed, the author himself may have been among the crowd of tourists on one of those days after the catastrophe.

Though sturdy, the box in which the recorder is housed is severely battered and scratched. On the outside of it, engraved by a professional hand, there appear a number of thus far undecipherable symbols: ⊕ , for which no explanation has ever been proffered; ⊗ , two triangles which have been variously interpreted as adaptations of the gyres of William Butler Yeats ° and representations of the yin and yang of Eastern mysticism; and ⊕ ,

---

° In the pamphlet, "The Ogden Lindwurmer Collection at Hughes." The anonymous author had clearly not played the tape.

perhaps affiliated with Zoroastrianism. None of these symbols, unless the yin-yang reading is correct, has any sound relation to either Eastern or Western dragon lore.

The document itself is strange but not entirely artless. The voice speaking into the recorder is somewhat dimmed by the age of the tape, but it appears to be that of a man of middle age with a pleasant and by no means histrionic manner, a man of good will and good humor, but with few of the refinements of the academy. In the box with the tape recorder and tape there is a curious letter written in what may be a feminine hand. The note is short and somewhat illiterate: "I fownd this box somewhere on the coast down near where I lived. The story sounds pretty good to me, so please Mr. Librarian put it in the library." It is unsigned. The note suggests that the tape recorder was actually mailed or delivered anonymously to the Hughes Library at some date shortly after the great quake. One suspects that the author was disguising his hand and his own erudition when he penned it.

Absolutely nothing more is known of the whole matter except that the recorder is of a kind sold in the late sixties at White Front stores along the departed coast.

Space is too short for a critical appraisal of the story here. The tale itself is obviously of the romance genre, with confessional structure. Perhaps it is best considered as a crude early contribution to the anti-romance movement that succeeded the anti-novel craze in the seventies. The author obviously transvaluates the ancient dragon myths and shows them no mercy. His scholarship is faulty and he cannot be excused for having corrupted the good work of J. F. Campbell, G. Henderson, T. W. Rolleston, J. Dragonette, J. Fontenrose, and other scholars in the field. The story itself has only a remote relation to contemporary life or to the history of dragon myths, and shows no sensitivity to the significance of dragons in dream symbolism. In this sense the book is as decadent as the other anti-romances of the period.

One thing more may be mentioned for the record. The box in which the plastic recorder resides seems to be the work of a blacksmith.

NEW NIXON, NEVADA
MARCH, 2001